Just Short Stories.

Patricia Jane Pitt.

The Author asserts her moral right under the Copyright, Designs and Patents Act, 1988, to be identified as the author of this work.

All Rights reserved. No part of this publication may be reproduced or copied. This book is a work of fiction. Names, characters and incidents are a product of the author's imagination. Any resemblance to people living or dead is entirely coincidental.

'Just Short Stories' Copyright 2016

Patricia Jane Pitt.

Contents

The Lay-By.
Stuck In an Elevator.
The Special.
The Job.
Albert's Bath Night.
Clutter Bug.
The Seaside.
The Charity Run.
The Abduction Of The Greyhound Cabbage.
Natas.
The Affair.
Ah! The pleasures of Kite Flying.
The Boy Who Floated.
Friday's Appointment.

Contents Continued.

Trust.
The News.
Letter To Claire.
Doing His Own Thing.
A Bit of A Giggle.
The Waiting Game.
A Slice of Life.
Jonathan Harris.
The Scarlet Thong.
Another Slice Of Life.
Best Friends.
The Bride.
Yet Another Slice Of Life.
The Murder Of Gareth Hughes.
A Fairy Story.
No Rival.

Dedicated to Derek. My love xxx

The Lay-By

Louise was desperate to spend a penny. She should have visited the loo when she called into the petrol station. However, as she was already behind time, she decided to wait until she reached the church where her friend was getting married. She prayed the church had a public convenience.

Driving along the dual carriageway, the pleasant scenery of Dartmoor whizzing by, Louise had a painful stomach ache. She had to relieve herself soon or there'd be an unpleasant consequence.

A few moments later, she spotted what she was looking for, a signpost, 'Lay-By. Half-a-mile'. She pulled into it, parked behind a council work truck, and noted several workers were cutting the grass verge at the side of the carriageway.

Stepping gingerly from the car, hoping not to cough, sneeze or do anything that would lead to a leak, Louise found once she had negotiated a bank and jumped across a stream, a wooded area allowed her the privacy needed to have a wee.

Checking no vehicle was about to pull into the lay-by and the council workers were still cutting grass, Louise went down the bank, jumped the stream then shot into the wood. Picking the largest oak for cover and all fingers and thumbs, she unzipped her blue trousers and pulled them, along with her knickers, down to her knees. Finally, she stooped to relieve herself of her heavy burden.

As she was about to pull up her knickers, she heard a rustling behind her. Turning quickly to face what had startled her and praying it wasn't one of the council workers, she was confronted by a dark-brown pony with eyes as big as golf-balls and long black lashes any girl would kill for.

Louise sighed with relief for she was thankful a pony had surprised her and not a person, but the pony turned quickly and kicked out at her. Louise sidestepped the pony but she had forgotten her knickers and trousers were around her knees. Consequently, she fell over and the pony raced off, whinnying.

After scrambling to her feet, Louise pulled-up her clothes and raced back to her car feeling a right twit. Her new blue outfit now moss and grass stained, and all because she didn't use the petrol station's facilities.

Therefore, the moral of this story isn't as you may think, make time to have a wee when you get the opportunity but, don't be caught with your knickers down because you don't know who or what might creep up on you.

Stuck In An Elevator

Sometimes life can be so annoying, especially when an elevator comes to a sudden stop. It was on one such occasion when I met Darrell. A bald-headed fat git who talked and talked the entire time we were stuck in it. Two hours, it had seemed like ten. When the elevator door opened, relief almost overwhelmed me for I wanted to drop to my knees and kiss the ground, but I fell into the arms of Joe, the elevator repair guy.

He was anything but a bald-headed fat git. In fact, he was ruggedly handsome with dark hair I wanted to run my fingers through. In addition, he was tall. Six two, I'd say.

"You okay, ma'am?" he asked in a deep, sexy voice.

"Yes," I squeaked. "But could you take me outside for some fresh air? I feel… weak." Well, I wasn't going to let a live one escape, particularly one like Joe.

"Certainly, ma'am," he said, giving me a lovely smile.

Not so much of the ma'am I wanted to say. It makes me sound old. I may not be a spring chicken, more a broiler, but hey, a girl must do her best in this climate.

As Joe led me away from the elevator, I glanced back at Darrell and wondered if I'd ever see him again. Cooped up with him for two excruciating hours, he'd told me his life's story. Boy, was it boring.

With only emergency lighting to see, he'd produced a

wallet full of family photos. First off, his wife, Sherrie, a plump, bottle-blonde haired woman. Then out came pictures of Wayne, Shane and Craig, his three overweight boys who ranged from seven to eleven. Handing me photo after photo, Darrell went into detail of why he'd taken it and where. Yet fate had played her part that day. Even though it had been unpleasant at times confined in the elevator with Darrell, he had told me his fantasy, to have it off in an elevator.

Since I don't let chances like that slip away, I obliged. In my line of work, a girl must earn her living when she can. Therefore, who am I to question other peoples' turn ons? In addition, seventy-five dollars helps pay the rent and these days I can't afford to be fussy.

Anyhow, I walked away from boring Darrell with Joe, his arm around my waist supporting me, my head resting on his broad shoulder. Joe looked as if he needed a mature woman to take care of him and do you know - he did! However, I'll tell you about that another time.

The Special

Gino's restaurant was just around the corner from Bartholomew's apartment. Bartholomew, a retired stockbroker, dined at Gino's every Tuesday and Friday evening at eight-fifteen. His corner table was always reserved for him and every time he entered the restaurant, Gino rushed to him and welcomed him like a brother.

Gino, a rotund man of sixty, had a way of making every customer feel special and his restaurant was renowned for its Italian cuisine. Gino now worked front of house, leaving the cooking in the capable hands of his two sons.

One Friday evening, as Gino showed Bartholomew to his table, Bartholomew said, "When are we going to have your delicious special? It's been ages since the last. And why do we have to wait so long?"

"Because my brother he only rears three pigs a year. But I have good news for you this evening." Gino's eyes sparkled. "Next week, my special will be on the menu. It is good news, yes? I already have my reservation diary full and, of course, your table is booked."

"I should hope so!" Bartholomew stated, placing his napkin across his lap. "Now, what do you suggest I eat this evening?"

"The pasta bake is particularly excellent, Mr

Bartholomew." Gino gave an exaggerated kissing gesture.

"Then as usual, I'll take your advice."

Gino smiled brightly. "You will not be disappointed and I shall bring you a generous portion. It will be with you very soon," he added, making his way to the kitchen.

That evening, as always, Bartholomew sipped his red wine while observing other guests. The restaurant was busy and all tables occupied, only one customer sat alone, a man. Bartholomew met his eyes and acknowledged him with a nod. The man returned the nod and smiled. Bartholomew had seen the man before but had not spoken to him. This suited Bartholomew because he didn't like conversation with anyone while dining.

Bartholomew believed that to eat while having a conversation was a crime against food. One should savour every morsel in silence was his philosophy. He actually thought about what he was eating. He chewed every mouthful until he had worked out every spice and herb it contained. Since dining at Gino's, Bartholomew's weight had increased to seventeen stone.

Ten minutes after Bartholomew's main course, Gino wheeled the tempting dessert trolley over to his table. "You're a dreadful man, Gino." Bartholomew waggled a finger at him. "You know I can't resist."

"I will take it away at once," Gino said, but didn't attempt to move.

"Go on then, I'll have just a little of that." Bartholomew pointed to a sherry trifle.

As usual, Gino piled enough dessert for two into the dish.

Bartholomew tutted. "You naughty man." Then picked up his spoon and ate the lot.

While draining the last of his red wine, Bartholomew's thoughts were still on food, the special. How many times had he eaten it? Six or seven, was it? He dabbed dribble from the corner of his mouth. Although he'd eaten a huge meal, his taste buds were watering in anticipation of next week's special. It was only meatballs. Nonetheless, they were perfection in a dish.

Bartholomew had asked Gino several times what the secret ingredient was that made his meatballs so delicious. Gino's reply was always the same. "I cannot tell you. My poppa he tells me and I tell my sons. It is, as you say, a family secret."

As Bartholomew rose to leave the restaurant that evening, Gino whispered, "Mr Bartholomew, I have surprise for you. My brother, he brings me the meat for my special dish. I know you have always been interested in how I prepare it, so as you are a good customer I shall let you see for yourself. Please, come this way."

"Gino, you do me a great honour," Bartholomew said, following him to the kitchen.

Gino stopped short of the doors and gestured for Bartholomew to enter first.

The kitchen was huge with stainless steel appliances and cooking utensils that shone. A long table ran down the middle, topped in stainless steel and edged with a gully.

Bartholomew turned to face Gino to tell him his kitchen was splendid but he came face to face with the lone diner he had seen earlier. "Ooh!... Where's Gino?" Bartholomew asked.

"He won't be long. He's attending to something in the restaurant. Please, sit down." The man indicated to a chair in the far corner of the kitchen.

As Bartholomew headed there, he felt a jab in the back of his neck. "Hey! What's going-" was all he managed to say before he collapsed onto the floor.

The man stood looking down at him. Bartholomew now paralysed.

"Being inquisitive is going to be the death of you, my friend. As you so eagerly want to know what the special is, I will tell you. Next week's special is you!"

The Job

I'd stalked him for weeks. He was so predictable it became boring. Monday through Friday, he worked in his office finalising the affairs of deceased clients. At twelve thirty, he spent an hour over lunch in one of the pubs scattered along the High Street. Sometimes he'd meet *her* and they'd hold hands across the table, smiling at one another.

His firm of solicitors dealt only with the wealthy and paid *him* over a hundred grand a year. That's my kind of man. One who earns good money.

His evenings were more eventful. He'd go to the cinema. Eat in expensive restaurants. Visit the gym or meet friends in clubs. He had a lifestyle I envied - and wanted.

During my stalking period, I put the first part of my plan into action. I went on a diet, changed the colour of my shoulder length hair from brown to blonde and bought a new wardrobe of clothes, similar to the ones he obviously liked on her, short, figure hugging dresses.

His girlfriend was tall, blond and slender. Blonde and slender, I achieved. The height was a problem but after weeks of wearing spike heels around my flat, I mastered the art of walking with my feet almost vertical. When I knew I'd catch his eye, I started the job. I bumped into him on purpose one night at a club, and as intended, I spilt my drink down my blouse.

"I'm sorry," he'd said.

"Don't be," I'd replied sweetly. "It wasn't your fault, it was mine." I then pulled out a handkerchief from my bag and mopped at the red wine adding, "This'll never come out but it'll teach me to look where I'm going in future."

"As I feel I'm partly to blame, let me pay to have it cleaned," he'd offered.

"That's kind of you, but no." I gave him a lovely smile. One of those I'd been practising for days, then I'd batted my long lashes at him.

"If you won't let me pay to have it cleaned, perhaps you'll let me pay in another way. Can I treat you to lunch one day next week? My name's Mark."

"That's very gracious of you, Mark. Yes, I'd like that, and my name's Emma." I reached for a paper napkin. "If you jot your number on that, I'll ring you sometime next week." I'd made sure I hadn't sounded too eager but inwardly I was ecstatic. Little did he know I now had my first step on his ladder.

I already knew his likes and dislikes. I'd done my homework. Following someone around for three months gives you a reasonable picture of his or her life. I'd even managed to get into his flat. I told his cleaner, "I'm glad I've caught you. I left my mobile in here last night. Can I look for it?"

"Don't see why not," she'd said. She went into

another room and I did some snooping. I whistled approval at his taste. Although it was sparsely furnished, what he had was top quality and state-of-the-art. I checked out his reading material and choice of music. I turned up my nose at both, but told myself I'd have to start reading crime fiction and listening to classical music.

I rang him, we had lunch, and although I gave him the come-on, he wasn't interested in me, so I wormed my way into his circle of friends.

Several weeks later, I poisoned his relationship with his girlfriend. Strange that people are ready to believe the worst about their loved one. I told Mark she was two-timing him. I set her up and made sure he saw her with one of his pals. I then gave Mark my shoulder to cry on and he became the proverbial, 'lamb to slaughter'.

Some weeks later, he asked me to move in with him, and then I really threw myself into my job. I eventually persuaded him to embezzle money from client's accounts. After twelve months, it totalled around two hundred thousand. I was surprised how easy it was for him to acquire twenty or thirty grand at a time. Of course, with inheritance tax and threshold duty being a maze of red tape, people expect and trust their solicitor to do things correctly. When some people inherit millions they don't check on where every quid went and have no idea they've been shortchanged. Those people want to grab the money and spend it, not worry whether their solicitor has ripped them off.

I must admit the first time he stole money I was scared. I answered every knock at the door with trembling hands. I expected to see the fraud squad.

We weren't stupid enough to keep the money in the flat, we rented a small security box at a local storage facility and every so often, I went and put money into it. When my nest egg was sufficient for me to live on comfortably for some years, I thought it was time to terminate my employment. I made Mark's life a misery by arguing with him for the least thing and I became difficult. I hoped he'd end our relationship but no matter what I did, he put up with it. Finally, I told him I thought we ought to part. He went ballistic. "If you leave me I'll tell the police what we've done."

I think he would have too. Therefore, I had to rid myself of him - permanently. My money waited for me and I wanted to spend it.

The day after he'd threatened me, I'd said, "You know I love you, Mark, and I'd never leave you. I was just being bitchy." I went and kissed him, passionately, and then we had sex. Afterwards, I suggested we went away for a few days to the coast.

The following week, while walking on a coastal path, I pushed Mark over the cliff.

Although killing him was never on the agenda, the rest of my plan went perfectly. I did have a few uncomfortable moments when the police grilled me. In spite of this, my act when I told them how he'd lost his footing would have won me an Oscar. I'd sobbed and said, "I'm devastated. I've lost the only man I'll ever love. How am I going to live without him?" It was obviously convincing because the coroner registered Mark's death as accidental.

After a show of mourning, I moved to Somerset, taking my money with me.

I made a little over four hundred thousand, in my opinion, not bad going for fifteen months work.

Albert's Bath Night

I wouldn't mind but she said your Albert did it. She stood there bold as brass and accused him. I said it couldn't have been him because he was having a bath at that time.

"And you know this for sure," she said in that condescending way of hers.

I squared up to her. "Of course I do. Friday night's bath night and at six o'clock it's Albert's turn to get in it. He's the forth-in line to bathe in our house and I remember clearly how the water was still reasonably clean after the other three had been in it. Therefore, he couldn't have done it if he was in the bathtub, could he?"

Anyway, I told her all this but could I convince her Albert hadn't done it. No. She'd have none of it.

Then, and listen to this, she had the nerve to say, "Perhaps you're mixed up. With the brood you have it wouldn't surprise me."

Can you believe it? Well, I stood my ground and although I shook with temper, I told her straight. "Just because you and your old man can't produce kids don't attack mine. My kids are good and I'm telling you for the last time, our Albert ain't done it, so there!"

She went off muttering and still accusing him of doing it. I watched her, hands on hips until she went indoors. What else could I do? I couldn't tell her he'd done it - could I?

 Sorry? What did he do? Ooh, the little bugger threw mud up her clean washing.

Clutter Bug

"This house is a bloody mess," Ray announced, coming through the front door. "Do you ever tidy it?"

Oh, God, I thought, he's visited his mother on the way home and she's had a go at him about me. "Yes I do," I said, kicking his trainers to one side. "But you don't help, do you? Your gym gear is where you dropped it last night. Can't you put it away instead of leaving it in the middle of the hallway?"

It all went down hill after that and another argument took place about the untidiness of our home. It happened on average once a week. Usually after he'd seen his mother, who was so house-proud she plumped up cushions and tidied around as guests left.

The day following our quarrel, I decided to de-clutter the downstairs. It seemed the in thing these days, de-cluttering the home. Clear out the junk and live with only what you need. De-cluttering will improve your life. At least, that's what presenters of those types of programmes say. They also say you can't go forward while having old clutter holding you back. Therefore, I thought I'd go for it.

I gathered Ray's out of date papers, magazines, books that had collected dust for years, and threw them in the recycling bin. I then put all the ornaments his mother gave us into a box, including the hideous clock she bought for our 21st anniversary, and then delivered the box to the charity shop. Because I'd caught myself one day dusting off his golf bag and clubs, which had stood in the corner of the living room for months, I took that too, also, his tennis racket and three pairs of trainers. That'll teach him, I'd thought. After all, we had a large garage where he could store his sports equipment. He didn't need to clutter up the living room with it.

By lunchtime, the room was de-cluttered. It appeared to have doubled in size. I then tackled the lounge. I dragged his battered old armchair and desk into the garden and set fire to them. They went up in flames without difficulty and to keep the fire going, I put on the pink fluffy cushions and pink rugs that his mother had bought us and which I hated.

By five pm, the house looked spacious. I could sit in armchairs without having to remove Ray's clutter first, and dusting would now be easy because there was only one ornament remaining in each room. On the mantelshelf in the living room, I left a vase of pink silk flowers. His mother had foisted these on me too. I propped the note I left for Ray against them.

I'd spent most of the night before my de-clutter thinking about my life and where it was going. Nowhere, I concluded. The past few years with Ray were difficult. Since our two children left home, we had grown apart and had nothing in common. He was into sport and out of the house five nights a week. He was living his life how he wanted and I decided it was time I did the same.

I knew Ray wouldn't approve of what I'd done that day. I'd written in my note, 'Ray. This is how I would like our home to look in future. Tidy and clutter-free. No longer will I allow your mother to rule my life by choosing what I should have in my home. If this is not satisfactory then I won't come back. Ring me on my mobile by seven this evening. Amanda.'

I wasn't upset when he didn't ring. So I checked into a B&B and the next morning I went to see a solicitor. The divorce was amicable. Everything dealt with fairly.

My life has turned out fine. Now I enjoy living alone with everything in its place and no clutter. As for Ray, I think he'll be content living with his mother.

The Seaside

"We came to Sutton-On-Sea for our honeymoon. Remember, Stan? We stayed in a place called Sandilands. I was ever so excited. It was to be expected, I was only eighteen. You moaned all week about how you hated the seaside. I loved it. I enjoyed walking along the shore barefooted. I liked the feel of the waves washing over my feet and the exhilaration I felt when the wind blew my hair. You complained about how your feet itched from the sand, so you vowed never to walk on the beach again, and you forbade me from doing so. We spent the remainder of the week in the local pub or in bed. That was forty-one years ago.

"Do you remember when we arrived home from honeymoon, Stan? You told your mother you'd never visit the seaside again. At the time, I didn't think you meant we would never go on holiday *anywhere* again.

"Are you comfy in the back, Stan? I bet you hate the fact I'm driving you because I know you detest women drivers. I've never heard you say a good word about one. Be assured though, I'll get us to our destination safely. As you know, I've done all the driving since you were ill, so I've had plenty of practice.

***

"Bloody hell, Stan, I nearly missed my turn. Sorry I pulled up sharp but I was so lost in thought, I reckon I would have driven straight to Lincoln if I hadn't seen that signpost. I'm glad the weather's fine. Forecast said it might rain later. I think I can remember this road, Stan. If my memory serves me correctly, this takes you into the centre.

"You know, I can remember every moment of our honeymoon. The white painted guesthouse with its blue gingham curtains and chintz covered armchairs, and the fantastic view of the wetlands we had from our bedroom window. Do you recall the bed, Stan? We laughed the first time we made love in it because it rocked its way into the middle of the room. You made it rock every night, even though I was in pain after you pushed me down the guesthouse stairs. That was the first time you were violent to me, on our honeymoon."

***

"We're here, Stan! Now we don't want to go to the town centre, we want to head for the beach. Ah! There's the road we need, vehicle access to the beach, half a mile. I expected to see more people milling about but then the season's nearly over. I think the place looks the same though, still quaint and old fashioned. I wonder if they still have donkey rides on the beach.

"Ah! There's the road leading down to it. I'll park as close as I can to the sea. You'll like that, Stan, won't you?

"Yes, I know! Remember to apply the brake. I have. I

don't want us ending up in the sea.

"Isn't this a good view, Stan? I can see several what look like tankers on the horizon. Can you see them? I'm pleased I thought to bring a flask and a sandwich. Just watching the waves coming and going is so relaxing and because the sea is all sparkly and inviting, I'm going to take off my shoes and paddle. You'll be okay until I get back, won't you?"

***

"Ooh, Stan, I feel wonderful now I've had that paddle, as if the wind has blown away my past heartache, and you did give me some. The worst, when you were unfaithful. How many times was it? Three? Furthermore, what about the time you punched me in the face, I couldn't go out until the bruising went. You said I deserved it, but I only took enough money out of your wallet to feed the kids. It wasn't as if I ever asked for much. Friends told me to leave you but where could I go? There weren't shelters for battered women in those days. Of course, I could have left a few years ago but you had that stroke and I was the only one who'd look after you. Your pals didn't want to know and the kids hated you so much they told me to wheel you to social services and leave you there. I couldn't do it. Guilt, I suppose. After all, you were my husband for better or for worse.

"In any case, it's time for you to get out of the car. I know you detest the seaside but for once, you're doing what *I say*. I know you wanted to be buried next to your mother but I have to get my revenge somehow. Therefore, scattering your ashes on the beach is my way of getting it.

"Another thing, I'm going to buy a bungalow in Sandilands so I can walk along the beach as often as I want. That way, I can trample over you as you did me. I told Alison this and she said, 'Do a return trip, mum, and trample on him for me'.

I thought that was really funny, Stan. So, as I've nothing more to say to you, I'll just take this lid off this cardboard box and scatter you at my feet. Bye, Stan. Away with you."

The Charity Run

"Only another three miles to go, Grandma," shouted a boy's voice from the crowd.

Is he having a pop at me? Sandra thought, groaning, for she was about knackered and still wondering what had possessed her to put her name forward to do a ten-mile run at her age. Reaching for the cup of water the marshal handed her, she told herself *she hadn't* put her name forward. Doris busybody Peters had.

Sandra started puffing as she went up a hill and was trying to focus on anything other than the three miles she still had to run. I'll never do it. Stupid idiot, she told herself, gasping. Jogging was for young things with good figures and firm breasts that didn't bounce up and down and hurt. She had tried holding her boobs flat at one point but felt silly running along with her hands clasped on them. She knew the extra weight that had crept on during the past few years didn't help. I wish I'd worn my shorts instead of these jogging bottoms, she thought, reaching the top of the hill.

"Cooie! Sandra!" Doris shouted. "I've come to support you and you're doing great. The W.I is ever so proud of you."

Sandra didn't reply. She just wanted to strangle Doris, very slowly.

Sandra was roped into taking part in the race. She had barely stepped through her front door after a week's holiday in Cornwall when the phone rang. "Hello, Sandra. It's Doris. I'm glad I've caught you and I hope you don't mind, but I've put your name down for the over sixties ten-mile charity run in aid of the local hospice. We wanted someone to represent the W.I. and you're the fittest."

"Me! Just because I walk a lot, it doesn't mean I can run, Doris. I'm sorry but it's out of the question."

"Oh, dear, I've already filled in the forms. You were away so we couldn't ask you but we hoped you'd do it."

Feeling pressured, Sandra had agreed to run. "And who else is taking part, Doris? *You*?"

"What with my bad hip."

"What bad hip? Didn't know you had one."

"Had it for years, love."

So now, after two months of training, well, jogging four miles at a time, the day had arrived and Sandra had her doubts about finishing. The stitch she had suffered at the four-mile marker was painful, then cramp got her at the sixth and she'd limped for quite a way, telling herself she wasn't a quitter. She wasn't, but she had never jogged more than four miles and now she was trying to do ten. Problem was not completing the race made her feel guilty. Her sponsorship money totalled a little over two hundred pounds and if everyone taking part raised that amount, it would be a tidy sum for the Hospice. With a huge sigh, Sandra soldicred on, even though her energy reserve was almost spent.

"Only another two miles, Grandma."

Who is that? Sandra wondered, glancing to where the voice came from. I bet it's one of those cheeky buggers off the estate come to catcall and make fun of us old ones.

Another two miles did he say? My feet'll never recover from this punishment. Ooh! Ah! Bloody hell! That cramps back.

"Don't give up, Grandma. Keep going."

Keep going? That's easy to say when you don't have to. *Who is it anyway?* She looked about her but could see only adults. The voice definitely belonged to a boy.

Sandra suddenly regained second wind. Her cramp went as quickly as it had come and her feet stopped aching. That's because they're dead, she told herself.

"Only one more mile, Grandma. I'll be waiting for you at the finish line."

She glanced to her left and this time saw a boy. A strange feeling crept over her as though everyone were moving in slow motion. Then into her mind sprang the beautiful face of her daughter Grace, who had died giving birth to a son, James, who had tragically died when he was seven. He'd be twelve now, Sandra thought, roughly the same age as the boy urging me to finish this gruelling race.

Into her head popped a notion. Is it James calling to

me? Am I going to drop dead at the finish line? Yes, that's it. I'm going to die at the end of this race and James will take my hand and transport me up to heaven to see Grace and my wonderful husband Mike. It'll be good to see him again. The idea of joining her family didn't upset Sandra. In fact, it spurred her on and gave her the extra stamina to finish the run.

"Come on, Grandma. You're nearly there."

"Okay," she said, racing to the finish line, where crowds of people gathered, bumping and jostling one another. Runners dropped to their knees, exhausted, and Sandra expected to keel over and witness the bright light of a near-death experience, which some people speak of. Nothing happened.

Then a boy ran towards her shouting, "Grandma. We're proud of you," but he ran past Sandra.

She turned to see him hugging a woman more or less her age. Sandra then realized the woman had run behind her throughout the race and the boy's words of encouragement aimed at *her*. I'm a foolish woman, Sandra told herself. Fancy thinking I was going to drop dead on the finish line. I bet lack of oxygen to the brain made me think so stupidly. Besides, I'm not ready to go yet.

"Congratulations," an official said, hanging a gold coloured medal around Sandra's neck. "How do you feel?"

"To tell you the truth, I thought I was a goner."

The official moved on, smiling.

Looking at her well-earned medal, Sandra felt a surge of elation and told herself, I've completed a ten-mile-run - at my age too, and her smile grew and grew.

The Abduction of The Greyhound Cabbage

Sam Johnson strode into his kitchen saying, "It's gone! Kidnapped. Right in front of me eyes."

"Don't be stupid, Sam," replied his wife Janet, who was preparing his cooked breakfast. "Who'd want to kidnap a cabbage?" Janet knew instantly what Sam was talking about. He hadn't spoken of anything else but his precious cabbage for days.

"I could name a few in this village who would like to kidnap it. I wouldn't be surprised if a ransom note isn't on its way right now."

"Really, Sam, you're getting paranoid about that cabbage." Janet flipped eggs in the frying pan adding, "It's only a cabbage for goodness sake."

"Only a cabbage!" Sam said, eyes opening wide. "It's not just a cabbage. I've sweated blood growing it. You don't realize what it meant to me."

"I do! That cabbage took over your life. If I'd have stood for it you would have slept with it in the bed and put *me* in the garage."

"Don't be stupid, woman. I wouldn't have asked you to do that. Maybe the guest room but never the garage."

Janet smiled at his remark.

"I still don't understand, Sam, why our village show is so important to you? It's only a minor one compared with the others you enter."

He sat down at the table and glared at his wife. "It may be a minor one to you but as far as I'm concerned it's the most important show of the year for me. Jack's been going on for days about what he's entering and Ray Barnes has been working on a secret formula for his brassicas and he's out to win."

Janet tutted. "The way you're acting anyone would think one of the grandchildren had been kidnapped. Now eat your breakfast." She plonked Sam's plate down in front of him.

"Eat! I can't eat at a time like this." Sam picked up his knife and fork. "To think that while I was having forty winks, someone entered the garage and snatched me cabbage. What's more, I was sleeping next to it. It took stealth to do that, I can tell you."

Janet sat down opposite him. "Are you sure you brought it from the garden last night?"

"Of course I'm sure. I'm not losing me marbles. When I carried it from the plot to the garage, I struggled me eyeballs out making sure I didn't bruise the leaves. No! It's been kidnapped."

Looking glum, Sam pushed a forkful of bacon into his mouth and while he scoffed his breakfast, he reflected on his cabbage. It was a beauty. The colour perfect, the leaves superb. He'd nursed it for weeks, tended it and spoke lovingly to it every time he saw it. He hadn't meant to brag about it in the Black Horse pub but it was the best Greyhound cabbage he'd ever grown. In his opinion, it would have won best in show. Now, it had gone, spirited away in the middle of the night. Who could have done such a dastardly deed? It couldn't have been me mates, he thought. They were too busy guarding their own specimens to try to nobble mine.

***

At two o'clock that afternoon, Sam and Janet wandered around Edingale show looking at the stalls. Sam's eyes narrowed with suspicion every time he saw an exhibitor who grew vegetables. Any one of them could have snaffled me cabbage, he thought.

As they headed for the marquee, Janet said, "For goodness sake put your face straight and enjoy the show. You look as if the world's about to end."

"I'm sorry but I just can't stop thinking about me little beauty."

"*Little*, did you say? That cabbage was a bloody monstrosity. Anyway, why didn't you enter your other cabbage? What was wrong with that one?"

"*What was wrong with that one*? Everything! That one was nothing compared with me little beauty."

"My, god, Sam, you're becoming a basket case. You're talking about that cabbage as if it were human. I think you're cracking up."

Entering the marquee, Sam shouted, "There it is, me Greyhound." He pointed to the winner's table.

"It looks more like a giant cabbage to me." Janet

giggled at her own remark. "And how do you know it's yours?"

Sam stared wide-eyed at his wife. "*How do I know it's mine*? How can you ask such a question? It's like asking if I could recognise one of me children in a room full of kids. Of course it's mine."

He went over to the winner's table and read the white card propped against the Greyhound cabbage. First Prize, Anonymous Entrant. He looked about the tent and saw one of the judges. "Excuse me, Mary. Can I have a word?"

"Of course," she replied, stepping over to him.

Sam tapped the white card with his index finger. "Anonymous doesn't tell us much, Mary. So how do we know who to congratulate?"

Her expression gave nothing away. "I know it's irregular but it is allowed. Of course, the judges have to know who entered all the exhibits but the public don't. So don't quiz me because I'm not telling you who entered it."

Sam frowned. He'd never heard or read about the anonymous rule and he'd been entering shows for years.

"Couldn't you give me a hint, Mary? After all, we've known one another a long time." Sam gave her a wink and a come-on-spill-the-beans grin.

"I just couldn't, Sam. I have my reputation as a judge to think of. Sorry." With a big smile bursting on her lips, Mary went off to mingle with other exhibitors.

After that, Sam told everyone he met that the prize-winning Greyhound cabbage was his and that someone had stolen it from his garage the night before.

Janet suggested they had a drink in the refreshment tent and when settled at a table, she said, "I can't stand it any longer. If you mention that damn cabbage one more time, I'm going to hit you over the head with a shovel. To stop me doing that, Sam, I'm going to tell you the truth. *I kidnapped it*! Some security guard you'd make. I still can't believe you spent the night with a cabbage in case something happened to it, which it did. I took it and you slept through it all. You were snoring five minutes after you'd bedded down. Therefore, for a laugh, I entered that cabbage in the show with Mary's approval."

Sam laughed. "I had an idea you were behind it but I must say," Sam pushed out his chest and polished imaginary buttons with his knuckles, "I knew me little beauty could do it. You know, I might have a go at growing melons for next year's show."

"No, you won't, Sam. If you think I'm going to take second place to a melon, you have another think coming. Next year you won't be here for the village show because we shall be on holiday. I shall make sure of it."

"Yeah, okay, whatever you say." However, Sam Johnson was thinking ahead. After all, he only had twelve months to raise another winner. A melon!

Natas

I read the newspaper article with interest. It read:
CORONER'S VERDICT FINALLY IN.

A coroner's inquest ruled today that 27-year-old Katie Rowlings took her own life. A postmortem revealed she had died from taking a huge amount of digitalis. The coroner referred to the rumours that some residents on the same floor as Katie had claimed she was murdered and believed witchcraft was the cause, but as no proof came forward to substantiate the residents claim, the coroner said he had no choice than to bring in a verdict of suicide while Katie's balance of mind was disturbed. The coroner made it clear he hoped today's verdict would end the speculation that she was murdered.

The newspaper reporter went on to write that a neighbour had alerted the police after not seeing Katie for several days and when they broke into Katie's flat, discovered her body slumped on a sofa. In her hand, a letter addressed to her mother. Katie had written, 'I don't want to live any longer. Please, God, forgive me'.

After reading the article, my thoughts lingered on Katie, for I had met her.

She had recently returned from the West of Spain, where for seven weeks, she learnt more about the black art. In a cavern, reached by a winding stone staircase, she studied with four other scholars. They saw no master and heard no reply to their endless questions. The answers they sought appeared on the cavern walls. Although there was no fee asked for their learning, they had to pay in another way. Pupils gave their body and soul to the great master, Satan. This, Katie had willingly done.

Katie had changed her name to Natas. People thought it was foreign but it was Satan spelt backwards. She knew he'd like that. When she left school at eighteen, she went to catering college and it was during this time she dabbled in the occult. It had started as a dare. She and a friend visited a medium and giggled throughout the proceedings. Then one night, during a wild party, someone produced an Ouija board and after she and several others played with it, Katie became hooked. She started to read about the occult and grew withdrawn and secretive.

Her parents tried in vain to get her to lead what they regarded as a normal life, but after countless arguments, she left home and didn't contact them again.

She somehow secured a council flat when she became pregnant. A few days after the birth of her son, she sold him to an American couple for fifty-five thousand pounds. The money quickly went. Learning the occult and joining in with devil worship is costly. Satan has a bank account, as anyone else, and his followers pay into it weekly. Vast amounts of money are needed in order for Satan to topple governments and conglomerates around the world. Her weekly subscription was seventy pounds. She paid it by cheque, making it out to Mr. S. Atan and sent it to a box number in Nottingham.

Paraphernalia littered her room. Jars containing living insects stood on dusty cupboards. Bird skeletons hung from the ceiling along with bunches of potent herbs as hemlock, monkshood, deadly nightshade and mandrake. All can hurt and kill. On a desk, stood an oil lamp, a large hourglass and a brass compass and scattered about the floor, quills and reams of ivory paper. Dozens of lighted candles rested on every available surface and on cobweb-laden shelves, old manuscripts written on parchment and edged with gold leaf, stood against spell books bound in black leather.

Although she claimed support for her and the son she sold, she didn't declare her income. She charged her clients forty-five pounds for reading their future with her Tarot cards. Nevertheless, she only used the powerful trumps. She could interpret the cards in any way she chose, usually to her advantage.

Every time she converted someone to Satanism, she believed Satan would, eventually, acknowledge her conquests and ask her to join his coven, where only the most privileged and supremely evil witches gather. They meet once a year in a small village near the New

Forest. After the human sacrifice, Satan appears and the orgy that ensues continues throughout the night. Natas anxiously waited for her master to test her devotion to him. She would not fail him whatever he asked of her.

She had just finished making a brew of Foxglove tea, enough to kill several people, when the doorbell rang. When she answered, she had no idea her test was about to begin.

He stood squarely in the doorway, slender and tall. His dark overcoat almost reached his boots and he wore a black trilby pulled well down. When he lifted his head, she looked into a pair of the bluest eyes she'd ever seen. "Come in," she had said. She knew he was a disciple of Satan even though she had not seen him before.

He did not enter. Instead, he placed his hands on her shoulders and she felt sharp fingernails dig into her back. He stared into her eyes and she became mesmerized when he began to speak. His voice was deep and chillingly quiet and he spoke in a language she hadn't heard before, but she understood every word. "Tomorrow evening a man will come to you at eight. He is a strong believer in the Tarot cards and he comes for a reading. This man must die before Saturday, so while under your spell, you must order him to take his own life on Friday. My master is depending on you, therefore, do not fail him."

"I will not fail him, and tell my master I will always do his bidding no matter what he asks of me," she had promised.

The man removed his hands from her shoulders, bowed his head in acknowledgement, turned from her and walked along the corridor towards the lift. He vanished before reaching it.

The following evening, she greeted her victim wearing a short-sleeved T-shirt and a skirt with a beaded hemline, which brushed the top of her docker boots. Numerous silver bangles jangled as she walked and every finger adorned with a ring. Her heavy eye make-up was as black as her clothes and matched her nail polish.

This is where I intervened. My name is Christabelle. Like Natas, I also dabbled in black magic in my younger days. Thankfully, a chosen one saved me. Since then, I have spent the past twenty years turning people from the black art to the white. It isn't easy. Particularly if they have achieved as much knowledge as Natas had. Nonetheless, she was beyond my help for she would never have turned from the dark side.

To be a true Wiccan and whose purpose it is to fight evil, one has to learn much about the black art. Many years ago, I also went to Spain and studied in the cavern. Even though it was difficult, I managed to stay focused on why I was there. I am now one of the elite. I have witnessed human sacrifice and seen much depravity.

Natas had gestured for me to sit, but she was already under *my* spell. She babbled on about how it was a pleasure to meet a member of the government. It surprised me she could not see past my facade and was actually speaking to a woman, not a man. The man she expected to read for was at home having dinner with his wife. Since she couldn't see I was a woman, I'd wondered whether to spare her life. Perhaps my elders were wrong. Maybe she wouldn't be as powerful as they believed. In spite of this, I remembered some of her activities during the previous ten months. How she had tried performing the black mass and had almost succeeded in bringing forth a black knight. Moreover, that October night in a local wood, where she'd cut the throat of a goat and drank its blood. She had not flinched and had laughed when the goat started fighting for its life, for her cut hadn't been deep enough. She watched its suffering without remorse. I was convinced her next sacrifice would be a child.

She was still talking when she reached for pen and paper. She neatly wrote, 'I don't want to live any longer. Please, God, forgive me.' She signed it Katie. Am I right to take her life? I had thought. Does this make me as evil as her? Yes! Even so, I had to stop her before she became too powerful. She would be, without doubt, a danger to humanity.

I mentally ordered her to take the bottle of Foxglove

brew from the shelf and drink it. She emptied the liquid into her mouth then flopped onto the black leather sofa. "You're in safe hands now, Katie," I had said, and I left her with happy thoughts from her childhood.

The Affair

"So did the earth move?" Greg asked with a smile getting up from the bed.

Marcia laughed. "My head spun a bit."

"Huh! You know how to make a man feel good."

Greg stretched, rotated his shoulders then looked at Marcia lying naked on her back.

"God! You look good enough to eat," he said, his eyes taking in her slender body. He sighed. "I wish I could spend more time with you today but Jayne's expecting me home early this afternoon." He bent and kissed Marcia's cheek, then ran his fingers through her long, auburn hair. "That man doesn't know what he's got. If I had a woman like you I'd never go astray."

Marcia laughed. "As far as I know he doesn't go astray. I'm fortunate." She gave Greg a smile. "And I'm fortunate to have you so come here and give me a kiss." She pulled him to her and they kissed long and hard.

Their affair had been going on for the past three years and as far as Marcia was concerned, that was how it would stay. She loved her husband and didn't intend to leave him. They had been married a little over twenty-five years and the spark was still alight between them. After their two boys left home, Marcia returned to full time employment.

While the boys were growing up, she had only been

able to work a couple of afternoons a week. However, her husband's job as a self employed painter and decorator had kept the wolf from the door. Yet full time employment for Marcia meant she and her family had the luxuries of life.

She had met Greg on the train into London one cold day in November. They struck up a conversation about the dreadful coffee from the refreshment coach and by the time they reached London, they'd arranged to meet later in the week. The past three years had flown and their relationship was strong.

Greg now made for the front door of the apartment. Marcia said, "I hate to mention this but the rent's gone up again. Can you pay another twenty?"

"Of course I can. You know I live for our meetings. It's what keeps me going." He put the extra cash on top of the eighty pounds he'd already placed on the dresser then blew her a kiss and was gone.

Marcia relaxed on the bed. She'd give herself ten minutes before getting ready for Gary. He was great fun and their two hours whizzed by. He always brought her a long-stemmed red rose - but she never took it home.

Ah! The pleasures of Kite Flying

I was flying my kite. Minding my own business. Wind perfect. Kite handling well. I was about to do a crossover when out of the blue someone shouts, 'Watch out, mate!'

Jumping at the sudden sound I spun round to see what was about to hit or mow me down. I couldn't believe my eyes. A rhinoceros was charging straight at me. Head down. Attack mode.

Have you ever been confronted by a charging rhino? No! I guess would be the answer.

So I ran. Straight for a gorse bush. Best of two evils, I'd thought. Headfirst, I dived in it. The rhino followed and tossed me into the air. I landed on his back. After bucking me off, he trotted away.

Therefore, the moral of this story is, fly your kite in a safe location and not in a Safari Park.

The Boy Who Floated

"Hey missus, give us hand." The voice belonged to Jacob, a boy of nine.

The missus was one Mrs Clegg, a haughty woman out walking with her Cairn terrier, Mr Jack.

"Hurry up, missus," Jacob said, wiping his runny nose on the sleeve of his worn-out blue jumper. "I need a drink."

Mrs Clegg looked nervously around but couldn't see anyone.

"Missus, I'm up here. In the air."

Mrs Clegg looked up. A nanosecond later, her eyes opened wide and her plump, bright-red lips fell open. Mr Jack started barking.

"Whatever are you doing up there?" Mrs Clegg asked. "Come down at once."

"That's the trouble, missus. I can't get down unless someone pulls me down. So give us hand will ya."

Mrs Clegg took hold of the boy's ankle and brought him back to earth. Because Mr Jack barked repeatedly, his barking shattered the peacefulness of the area.

"He's a noisy bleeda ain't he, missus?" Jacob said, steadying himself like a sailor trying to get his land legs. He gave his nose another wipe on his sleeve before adding, "Don't it drive ya nuts? Him! Barking like that."

"But that's what dogs do. He's a good boy though,

aren't you, Mr Jack." Mrs Clegg bent down to ruffle his brown and white shaggy hair. "Now be quiet," she told him, but Mr Jack continued to bark.

Jacob couldn't stand it a moment longer and gave him the most piercing look. Mr Jack instantly shut up and lay down, looking as though Jacob had turned him to granite.

Mrs Clegg pulled up straight. "So why couldn't you land?" she asked, as if seeing a boy floating in the air was a regular occurrence in those parts. Those parts being the Wye Valley and she was out on her afternoon walk along the river with Mr Jack.

"Because the angel told me if I land meself I'll lose me powers and I don't wanna lose 'em." Jacob took a small rucksack from his back and opened it. After ferreting inside, he brought out a small bottle of Tango and a packet of cheese and onion crisps.

Mrs Clegg said, "So young man, what's your name and where do you live?"

"Me name's Jacob and I live in London," he informed her while unscrewing the bottle of Tango.

"Good gracious. You haven't floated all the way from there today, have you?"

"I have. Sometimes I cross the channel and spend a day in France. It's ace!"

Mrs Clegg opened and closed her mouth like a landed codfish. "I simply can't believe what I'm hearing. Wait until I tell the Women's Gild about this. I bet they will not believe it either. So, Jacob, how did you get your power of flight?"

Jacob sat down on a huge boulder and opened his crisps. "It was like this, missus," he replied, stuffing a big crisp into his mouth. "I was fast asleep one night and something woke me. I opened me eyes and a mist appeared, a big ball of it. Slowly the mist took the shape of me dead granny. She wore Victorian clothes and had her hair all coiled on top of her head. She had a beard too!"

Jacob laughed loudly at his recollection before continuing with his story.

"Now, although I knew it was me granny, she looked different to when she were alive. Me dad said in her younger days she was a dolly bird, whatever that means, but when she got older she turned into an old tart; I dunno what that means either. Anyway, the mist disappeared and it was me granny come back as an angel. Stroking her beard, she said, 'Now, Jacob, because you've been a good boy and looked after your mother while she was ill, I'm giving you the special power of floating'.

"I said to her but granny I can do that already because I can swim real good. She made a cackling sound like a witch before saying, 'Not floating in water, silly, floating in the air, but you must listen to me very carefully, Jacob. You can float anywhere you like, even to the other side of the world. But you must not touch down on land without someone's help or the spell will be broken and you won't be able to float anymore'. So that's it, missus. Since last week, I've floated everywhere. It's ace! And I ain't bin to school since."

"My word, Jacob, that's a strange story. But you should go to school, young man." Mrs Clegg gave him a stern look. "You will need your education for the future."

"Actually, I might go tomorra. It's gymnastics and I like that."

Jacob took a swig of his Tango and stood up, brushing dirt from the back of his scruffy blue jeans.

"Well, gotta go, missus. Eastenders is on telly tonight and I don't wanna miss it." He threw his empty crisp packet to the ground, returned the Tango to his rucksack, put his arms through the straps then rose effortlessly into the air. "Bye, missus."

"Goodbye, Jacob, and please take care up there."

She still spoke to him as if a floating boy was the norm in the Wye Valley. She gave him a wave, bent and picked up his rubbish then continued on her way along the path. Mr Jack walked quietly by her side and Mrs Clegg had no idea at that moment that he would never bark again.

Friday's Appointment

She lived in a terraced house in Stoke-On-Trent and had few pleasures. She had five kids and getting them ready for school took most of her energy. She'd return home from walking them to school to find her husband had crawled out of bed and was snoozing on the worn-out sofa. She would watch his fat belly rise and fall as he drew breath and she'd ask herself what she had done to deserve such a depressing life.

She was tall and thin, owing to her not eating enough. She'd go without food so her kids wouldn't go hungry. Her pretty smile had faded over the years and was now lost, and her limp brown hair hung untidily about her shoulders.

She met her husband when she was sixteen and he eighteen. He hated his parent's hand-to-mouth existence and wanted to better himself. He'd been full of dreams of how to achieve a prosperous lifestyle and she'd been swept along on his enthusiasm. A few months after they started dating she found herself pregnant. Then the dreams ended.

They had married at the registry office, lived with her mother until the baby was born then had moved to their back-to-back. Now, twelve years later, they existed on benefit and she hoped the loan shark would never call in his marker.

He came on a Friday morning at eleven and rattled

the letterbox. When she opened the door, he would greet her with a cheery hello and talk about the weather. Yet once inside her drab home, they'd go upstairs and he would almost rip off her clothes then climb on top of her. She'd stare at the yellowing ceiling and peeling wallpaper and try to think of nothing until he was satisfied and spent. Every Friday followed the same pattern. Her husband went to the bookies and the loan shark called.

It had started some years back with a fifty-pound loan to help cover costs over the Christmas period. Then a hundred, then two, and now they owed so much she knew they would never get out of debt. Her husband never queried how she found the money to pay the loan shark. She often wondered if he knew and allowed it to continue by way of unspoken agreement. Paying off the loan shark this way, had become a way of life to her.

He arrived one Friday, breathless. He asked for a drink of water. As she handed it to him, she hoped he would choke on it. He didn't but during his frenzied climax, he suffered a heart attack. She watched him die and felt nothing. Not a flicker of compassion or regret appeared in her dull, brown eyes. She pulled up his trousers, shoved him into his jacket and wrote 'Paid in Full' across her debt in his notebook. She then dragged him downstairs, threw him into a chair and rang 999.

Some months after the loan shark died, she watched

her husband lying spread-eagled on the sofa watching telly. She'd had enough. Things had to change. She filled the washing-up bowl with cold water and threw it over him. He shot up from the sofa and went to hit her.

"Don't you dare," she said. "Because if you do I'm gonna kill you the same way as I killed the loan shark." Her husband looked puzzled but she knew she had his full attention. His hand hovered then fell to his side. "What I used on the loan shark wasn't detected, was it? So, I warn you, you'd better mend your ways or watch what you eat."

He looked confused; she inwardly smiled. Something told her their life would now change and maybe some of those dreams could turn into reality after all.

Trust

I decided to kill him when he leaned across the café table and kissed her. She was attractive, auburn haired and at least half his age.

It was pure chance I walked past the café that evening. I normally go straight home after pottery lessons but that week I thought I'd do a little window-shopping. I wandered along the high street and the lingerie shop grabbed my attention. On display was what I was looking for, a full-length, aquamarine silk nighty. Perfect for our romantic weekend in London, I'd thought. We had booked a suite at the Savoy and seats for 'Dirty Dancing' to celebrate our silver wedding.

My thoughts were on the delicate nightdress as I walked past the café. Something made me stop and I glanced in. Their foreheads were almost touching and they were laughing and seemed unaware of anyone. I watched them and when he kissed her, I felt I was doing something I shouldn't, so I stepped away. I leant against a wall, legs wobbly. I couldn't think straight. Anthony was seeing another woman and this time I had no idea.

I heard the ting of the café's doorbell and darted into a doorway, hoping it wasn't Anthony and his latest lover. It was, and I prayed they wouldn't walk my way. They didn't; they stood outside the café.

She said, "So your wife doesn't suspect?"

"No. So when shall we meet again?"

"How about next Monday at the George Hotel? Around eight."

"That's fine," he agreed, kissing her cheek.

He arrived home after me. I said, "I tried ringing you earlier but got no reply."

"That's strange because I haven't budged from the office all evening. Perhaps the phone's playing up again."

Lying came easily to him. Not a flicker of guilt crossed his face, so right there and then, I decided to kill him. He'd sworn the last time I caught him cheating he'd never be unfaithful again. If I killed him, he wouldn't be able to.

During the weekend, I was so attentive to him it made me inwardly squirm. Watching him eat his Sunday lunch, the solution to how I was going to kill him came to me. I'd poison his dinner on Monday, then go and confront *her*.

I made curry and as we sat eating it he remarked, "This is the best you've ever done, love. You've put something different in it though, haven't you?"

"Yes. But I'm keeping it a secret," I replied, taking another forkful of mine. I couldn't very well tell him I'd sprinkled a cocktail of poisons over his portion, could I? He ate the lot and even asked for seconds. Anything to oblige, I thought, serving him another helping.

He said, rather lovingly actually, "I'm looking forward to our weekend away. And I've a surprise for you."

"And I've one for you," I told him, watching him pop the remainder of his curry into his mouth.

He smacked his lips. "That was delicious."

"Good, since it'll be your last."

"Last?" he queried.

I smiled at him. "Only because that one took me ages to prepare so I doubt I'll do another."

After I'd done the deadly deed, I put on the red dress I'd bought especially for London, spent ages with my make-up and hair and when I was satisfied with my appearance, I went to meet *her*.

I left *him* slumped in his armchair gasping for breath. I guessed he was having a heart attack. To make sure he couldn't summon help, I cut through the landline cable and took his mobile. I wasn't bothered about what the post-mortem would reveal. I'd endured a rotten life at times with him so I didn't care. Besides, I had photographic evidence of Anthony's beatings and had seen a solicitor about his behaviour in the past. I had considered leaving him several times. Unfortunately, I fall into the category of foolish women who stupidly believe their man when they beg for forgiveness and swear never to hit you again. When he wasn't cheating on me or beating me up, he was loving and kind. During those times, life was good. Nevertheless, his latest affair was as they say, 'the last straw'.

She sat in a far corner of the George Hotel looking smart in a black fitted suit. I went straight over to her and smiled. "Hello, I'm Anthony's wife. I'm afraid he can't make it this evening. He's been taken ill."

"I'm sorry to hear that. Nothing serious, I hope."

"Just a touch of food poisoning," I said, sitting down opposite her.

"Ooh, nasty. Let's hope he's feeling better soon. In case you don't know, my name's Julia. Can I get you a drink?"

"Thank you. I'll have a red wine."

She called the barman over and ordered my drink and a coffee for herself. I was astounded at how relaxed she appeared at meeting me.

Once the barman had placed our drinks on the table, she delved into her black handbag, brought out a small silver box, opened it and handed me a sapphire and diamond ring.

"Try it on for size. I assume you know about it as you're here." She gave me a lovely smile before adding, "Anthony did worry about our meeting one another in case you found out and jumped to the wrong conclusion."

"So… Er… you aren't having an affair with Anthony then?"

"Certainly not! My dad and Anthony play golf together and dad happened to mention to Anthony that I'm a jeweller, so he asked me to design and make a ring for you for your silver wedding. We met at night because it was easier for me."

I stood up, snatching the ring. "If only he'd told me," I said, racing to the door.

"But he wanted to surprise you," she called.

"He did!" I shouted back. "And I surprised him too!"

The News

When I heard the news, my reaction was to tell him as soon as he came in from work, but he wouldn't be home for another four hours so this gave me time to think about it. Should I tell him tomorrow over dinner at one of our favourite restaurants?

He loves Carlo's place. He says his pasta dishes are the best he's eaten. He'd know because he dines at some of the finest restaurants. It was at Carlo's he proposed. I couldn't believe it. Out of his jacket pocket, he produced a diamond solitaire ring. No theatricals, he isn't showy like that. No hearts, flowers or violins, he just asked me to marry him. I said yes. That evening was the first time we made love.

Shall I tell him on one of our walks? Perhaps tonight, after we've eaten. We often take a stroll around the village where we live. It now looks vibrant with everything bursting into life. The daffodils edging the verges are particularly strong and colourful this year. It was on one of our strolls, I told him I was pregnant with twins. He shed a tear and said I'd made him happier than he ever thought possible. He doted on his daughters' right from the moment they were born. Still does, and spoils them.

Maybe I should tell him the news in Cornwall. Suggest we take an impromptu break. We could go to our tiny white-painted cottage we bought six years back. We've had wonderful times there, just the two of us. We usually arrive on a Friday evening after flying to Cornwall in his plane. After landing, a taxi takes us the ten miles to our get-away-from-it-all cottage, located fifteen miles from St.Ives. From the moment we reach the fishing village, we enjoy a weekend of bliss. He unwinds after a busy week in the city with the help of a bottle of red Bordeaux; I enjoy a bottle of white. We drink until tipsy then tumble into bed.

Late on Saturday morning, we go down the steep hill into the village and eat fish-and-chips on the harbour wall. Making our way back, hand in hand, we stop and speak with everyone we meet. While unlocking the cottage door, his hand usually strays to my bottom and he cheekily squeezes it. I giggle like a schoolgirl at his touch.

After making love, I drift back down to earth, feeling save and loved, his strong arms around me. Being with this man who shows me such tenderness is beyond words. There were times at the cottage I revelled in a daydream. I imagined we were having a secret love affair.

I have fond memories of Cornwall. No! Telling him my news at the cottage won't do. It'd be heart breaking and would spoil what we had there. I couldn't mar it with such news.

From the moment I met him, I felt a bond between us. He told me he felt it too.

He had stood chatting with a group of people and as I'd offered them a drink from my tray, his eyes had met mine and that's all it took for me to fall in love with him. I was in my last year at university and working that night as a temporary waitress.

After finishing work, I was heading down the conference centre steps when a deep velvety voice called, "Helen! It is Helen, isn't it?"

I turned and there he was, the man whose eyes had met mine.

We married eleven months later. My mother still says, 'Helen, that New Zealander swept you off your feet'. He did! He's twelve years older than I am and very successful in the world of advertising.

I don't want to tell him the news because I can already picture his face. The deep frown will appear first, followed by a look of disbelief. Then he'll cry. I know him so well you see. He'll give me the look, the expression that says I'm sorry. I've seen it before when he cancelled arrangements at the last minute. We'd be about to go out and the phone would ring. "Sorry. Business. Gotta go!"

I did wonder if he had another woman and I'll admit there were times I grew suspicious when he had to go out unexpectedly. I'll own up, I did ring the office on more than one occasion when suspicion got the better of me, but he was always there. You'd probably check too if your tall, dark and handsome man went out at a moment's notice, particularly if he used the old clichés, 'Sorry, Darling. Business calls. Don't wait up'. The faithful wife has no idea that hubby is going out to have it off with a younger, more glamorous woman. I'd know; my husband's eyes would betray him.

He meets high-flying businesswomen most days and some look as though they've just stepped from a top-notch fashion magazine, dressed to impress and some to allure. Perhaps he's been tempted? Possibly. However, I know there isn't another woman for him because from the moment we met his every act, word, touch and glance, has proved and shown how much he loves me.

This morning when he left for work, he whispered seductively, "Bye, Darling. See you this evening. Take care. Love you."

His lips lingered on mine for longer than usual. Even now, he still brings on butterflies in the pit of my stomach with just a look of his bewitching brown eyes. With a parting kiss to my cheek, he ran down the porch steps and got into his car.

As he pulled out of the driveway, I told myself I had a lot to be thankful for. I'd had a stress-free marriage, had two beautiful girls, and been given the best of things. What more could a woman ask for?

Then early this afternoon, *he* knocked my door. When I opened it, he greeted me with, "Hi there! Are you Mrs Taylor?"

I nodded and thought, he's a salesman, but before I had chance to tell him I didn't need anything, he flashed a badge and handed me a business card.

"I'm Terence Wright, Mrs Taylor. A private detective and I need to speak with you on an important matter."

He looked respectable in his smart blue suit, blue shirt and tie, and he carried a bulging briefcase. I obviously appeared concerned because he said, "Please ring this number, Mrs Taylor." He tapped the business card. "It's the London branch of the detective agency I work for. They'll vouch for me. I'll wait here while you call them."

I did, and Terence Wright was who he said he was, a private detective. Of course, it could have been a set-up but everything about it seemed right, so I asked him in.

We sat in the conservatory. He looked uneasy and fidgeted in his seat. He drew breath to speak several times but held back looking as if he didn't know where to begin. I offered him a drink of water but he refused.

"So then, Mr Wright, what's this important matter?"

He cleared his throat. "The man who calls himself Alexander Taylor is in fact Terence Wright - my father."

"I beg your pardon?" I said.

"I'm sorry to have put it so bluntly but he abandoned my mother and me when I was seven months old."

My first reaction to this man's revelation was to say

you have it all wrong, but something held me back and I let him continue.

"Over the years, my mother and I have often wondered what had become of my father. Some months back I decided to find out. After he abandoned us, he came to England, changed his name, had a little cosmetic surgery then climbed the corporate ladder before striking out on his own. As yet, I have not informed my mother of my findings and I know she will be as shocked as you when she learns he's married, since she never divorced my father and he sure never divorced her."

My stomach lurched as the word *bigamy* shot into my head. For the past twenty-three years, I had lived with a bigamist. The realization my marriage was a sham made my insides churn, but I managed not to throw up.

What Terence Wright said could have been questionable but before he even went on to show me proof I knew he was Alexander's son. He had his bewitching brown eyes. Terence went on to tell me he lived in New Zealand with his wife and two boys and that he made a good living working for the detective agency. Although Terence wants to confront his father, he has promised he won't approach him until I have spoken with him first.

So, when do I tell Alexander my news? Tonight? Tomorrow? Never?

Letter To Claire

The Limes
September

Dear Claire,
I'm sorry about the long delay in replying to your last letter, but things here have been hectic. I haven't had a minute to myself. Thank you for the letter opener you sent me for my birthday. Being solid steel, it'll last for years and it's very sharp. I've used it on many occasions but I have to admit, not for its proper purpose. I'm still sliding my thumb into envelopes and giving myself those nasty paper cuts because I keep your versatile gift in the side pocket of my new armchair. That reminds me, I can bring it out from there now. You see, I used to poke him with it when he started snoring. It's because of his snoring we're getting divorced. Oh, of course, you don't know. I'll tell you about that later.

I'll answer your questions now. Yes! Linda is still having her affair with Stuart. His wife must be an idiot. If your Jeff went out almost every night without you, wouldn't you become suspicious? Some women are thick. Mind you, if I were married to Stuart I'd be glad to get rid of him. I must tell you this. Joanne got so drunk at her daughter's twenty-first she fell against one of the buffet tables and knocked it over. You should have seen the mess. Fresh cream sponges, trifles and dozens of cupcakes went everywhere. Maxine ran crying from the room screaming, "I hate you, Mum. You've ruined my night." Although it was embarrassing, I couldn't help but smile, you'd have enjoyed it too!

And yes, I'm still attending my art class. The guy who runs it is rather dishy. He's the classic, tall, dark and handsome type. He lives with another guy in one of those apartments by the train station. Do you remember Alan Aldridge? He was the man who ran off with Pam, the church organist's wife. Well, Alan's back in the village and living with - you'll never guess. Caroline! Apparently, she went to visit Pam in her love nest with Alan and if my memory serves me correctly, it was the other side of Lichfield. In any case, Caroline went several times and one day, Pam came home early from work and caught Caroline and Alan in bed. Talk about the cat amongst the pigeons. Still, I don't know how he can show his face in this village after what he did. Some people have a nerve. I haven't found out what's happened to Pam but when I do, I'll let you know.

Give Jeff my regards and tell him I hope his varicose vein operation won't be too painful.

Now, onto *my* news. I've bought one of those motorised armchairs. It's dark-grey and so comfortable I've slept on it at night because when extended it's like a bed. Of course, when he tried it he wanted one but he went and bought a better one. His had a lift-up tray on one side, so he could put everything he needed on it in order to watch the TV. Things like remote control, cigarettes, ashtray and glass of whisky. You should have seen him lazing in his brown leather armchair acting like the lord of the manor. I wanted to hit him.

Anyhow, his chair was the reason why things started to deteriorate between us and why we're getting divorced. Almost as soon as he turned on the telly, he nodded off. I know everyone is entitled to doze in the evening but most times, we'd argue about what to watch on the box. Of course, he always won the battle because you know me, anything for a quiet life. Then, typical, minutes after his programme started he was snoring. I'd switch to another channel but moments later he'd shout, "Hey! I was watching that. Switch it back." Therefore, I decided if I had to watch his choice of viewing, he was going to watch it too. That's when the poking began. Every time he started snoring during his must watch programme, I prodded him in the arm with the tip of the letter opener. Arguments started about it and you should have heard his language. It was awful. He threatened to stab me with it if I didn't give over but I kept telling him, "You stop snoring and I'll stop stabbing."

This went on for some time and I will confess I started prodding him harder. I enjoyed it too! One night, I really gave it to him. He was fast off so I leaned over and jabbed him in the ribs with it. Before I had time to square myself back in my chair, he jumped awake, shot out his arm and hit me in the face. Consequently, with *my* delicate skin, within hours, my face looked like someone had hit me with a baseball bat, so I went to a solicitor and told her my husband had beaten me up.

To cut a long story short, I got a restraining order against him for his violence so he had to move out. Our divorce should be finalised in a week or two. Of course, the house is already on the market since he wants his share. I'll write and give you my new address once I've moved from here.

Well, that's about it for this time. Thank you again for your gift. It's the best present I've ever received. Write soon. Love from me to you. xxx

Doing His Own Thing

"Arthur, I want to talk to you. What I'm about to say will come as a shock so you'd better sit down."

Arthur sat at the kitchen table and looked at his wife, who stood with her back to the sink, arms folded across her chest.

"I'm leaving you, Arthur. No! Don't interrupt. As you know, we haven't had a real marriage for years. It's time to call it a day and get a divorce. The best way to end it is for you to keep the house and I'll have the savings. That's fair I think."

"Very fair, May," Arthur replied, and hoped his inner feelings wouldn't betray him. He felt ecstatic. In his early fifties, he had prayed for May to bugger off. God had finally answered those prayers, he told himself. He could now do his own thing but he'd better look a little hurt, but not too much. He didn't want her to feel guilty and change her mind. "What's brought this on, May?"

She came and sat opposite him. "I'm not leaving you for another man. Or a woman," she laughed. "I want to travel. But I don't want to do it with you."

"Right. So when are you leaving?"

"Saturday. I'm renting a flat until everything's settled. Then I shall buy a small bungalow on the coast. You seem to be taking it well, Arthur. Aren't you bothered?"

He thought he'd better make an effort. "Of course, I am. After all, we've been married forty-three years."

"Yes, Arthur, but let's be honest the past twenty-five have been loveless."

True, he thought, but when your wife says on her forty-second birthday, 'Arthur, I don't want intercourse again because I don't like it', love ebbs away. Moreover, once May made up her mind about something she wouldn't change it. Although Arthur felt deflated when she announced sex was off the menu, he wasn't too bothered because for a long time he felt he'd been trying to make love to a slab of marble. As their love for one another had gone off the boil, they started leading separate lives. He played snooker at the British Legion three times a week, tended his landscaped garden and redecorated when needed. May went to flower arranging classes, took up indoor bowling and became a churchgoer. For years, this was how they spent their time.

Jenny had entered Arthur's life eighteen months previously. She was a merry widow full of vitality. Their affair had started innocently enough. He was playing snooker one evening and she challenged him to a game. She won, and afterwards they had a drink together. The following week they played again and he walked her home. He kissed her cheek and said goodnight. On the second occasion, she invited him in.

One kiss led to another, then they were making love on her four-poster bed and Arthur thought he was in heaven.

As time went by their lovemaking hit the heights. Jenny was anything but a slab of marble and got herself into positions he never thought possible. He often wondered if she was a contortionist, as he lay gasping for breath on the bed after strenuous sex.

"Arthur! Are you listening to me?"

"Yes, May." He wasn't. Even though he'd watched her lips move her words hadn't reached his ears. He was mentally tapping himself on the back and thinking how lucky he'd been to get away with adultery. It wouldn't matter now if May found out because she was leaving him and he could do his own thing.

Do his own thing, he thought. Hadn't he been doing that for years?

Reality hit!

Oh, God! Who'd cook his meals, wash his clothes and generally take care of the day-to-day running of the house? He felt his ordered life begin to crumble. He didn't love Jenny and she was useless around the house. May could deal with anything but Jenny flapped at the slightest problem and cooking? Hers was awful. He now realized why his life was easy; May was his backbone.

When sex and lovey-dovey went off the menu, Arthur had questioned himself why he stayed with May. *Now he knew why.* Other than her denying him sex, his life at home was comfortable. They were mortgage free. They hadn't any debt. Their daughter was happily married and May was a good woman. She never squandered money or bought frivolous items, was a fantastic cook and kept the house immaculate.

He was about to plead for May to stay when he caught the word Jenny. "Er… What did you say, May?"

"I said you can now see Jenny anytime."

"I don't know what you mean."

"Of course you do. I've known about your relationship with her for ages. I can see you're surprised but for goodness sake, Arthur, you can't have an affair in the village you live in without some one noticing, but I'm not bitter. I was expecting you to leave me but you kept coming back. I was hoping you'd ask for a divorce. So now, I'm asking you for one. Well, telling you."

"But... But..." was all he could say. He was reeling from her words and the fact that she had said them without feeling.

"By the way, and I don't like kicking a man when he's down, but you do know Jenny is also having an affair with Eric, don't you? Want a cuppa?"

That night, Arthur went to the local pub and sat alone in a corner contemplating his life. What was to become of him? He'd never cope without May and Jenny was unfaithful to him. What hurt him most was the fact May wasn't leaving him because of his adultery; she was leaving because she didn't want to spend the remainder of her life with *him*!

Finishing his pint of bitter, he stood up and left the pub. He didn't return home. He went to the railway crossing and stood in front of the nonstop train to Birmingham. He was doing what he had always done, his own thing.

A Bit of a Giggle

"Go on, be a devil," Sylvia had joked. "You never know, I might get in touch with Fred. See how he's coping with the Afterworld. Perhaps he's getting on better there than he did here. I'll be able to ask him."

Sylvia told me numerous times she didn't love Fred but she went ahead and married him. When he died, rather suddenly, he left her pots of money.

"No need to work now, is there?" Sylvia had remarked, handing in her notice.

After much brow beating, she had finally talked me into going to the medium's house and taking part in a séance.

"It won't kill you," she'd laughed, as we waited for the front door to open. "It'll be a bit of a giggle."

I often think of that séance and the events that took place that night.

An old man had eventually creaked open the door and beckoned us to follow him. He had led us into a dismal room where five people sat round a circular table; in the centre, a candle flickered casting eerie shadows on the dingy walls. "Isn't it a hoot?" Sylvia had giggled, and then giggled more when the old man showed us to our seats.

He had explained what was about to happen and insisted under no circumstances were we to move from the table or release hands once the séance started. It was essential to maintain the circle and allow the spirits to enter freely.

The medium had then begun chanting in a low voice.

I'd looked across at Sylvia expecting to see a smile on her perfectly made-up face. There wasn't. Her eyes, large as gobstoppers, were fixed on the medium. The other people around the table sat in a deep trance.

When the medium asked, "Is there anybody there?" I'd felt a blast of cold air on the back of my neck and I'd shivered.

Then I started to tremble when I heard, "Sylvia... Sylvia." The deep voice cut through the deathly stillness of the room.

I watched Sylvia slowly move her gaze from the medium to where the voice called. Her vivid blue eyes had portrayed terror when she asked, "Is that you, Fred?"

"Who else? Love of my life."

"W-what do you w-want?" Sylvia had stammered.

Fred had laughed. "You know the answer to that, Sylvia, don't you?"

In a panic-stricken voice, she'd shouted, "No! I don't want to go with you, Fred. I mustn't break the circle. Please, let go of my hand."

Turning my head to face the doorway, I'd seen Fred dragging Sylvia from the room. I'd wanted to call to them but couldn't find my voice. Then I looked across the table and relief had engulfed me. Sylvia was still sitting in her chair.

The medium finally ended her chanting and came out of her trance.

As the room grew brighter, my senses flooded back. What had I seen in that room? I'd wondered.

I remember rising unsteadily from my chair and on wobbly legs, skirting the table and making my way round to Sylvia.

"I'm sorry," the medium had said. "Your friend has left us."

"Don't be silly. She's sitting here," I'd replied, tapping Sylvia on the shoulder.

"You misunderstand. I mean her spirit has left us."

I gave Sylvia a good shake saying, "You've had your giggle so stop messing about."

But she was dead!

I found out a couple of weeks later that Fred died from falling down the stairs. Was it an accident? Or, was he pushed? I also learnt Fred secretly went to the same medium Sylvia and I had visited. Strange isn't it? Still, it was only for a bit of a giggle. Wasn't it?

The Waiting Game

Sara hung out her washing feeling as happy as a schoolgirl. That evening, she was going to give Andy what he wanted and what he'd patiently waited for. *Her*!

As Sara pegged a black thong on the line, a picture of the evening ahead shot into her mind. She'd serve Andy melt-in-the-mouth vol-au-vents filled with creamed mushrooms, served with cheese-topped crusty bread. Second course, prime rib with all the trimmings and tiramisu for dessert and all of it accompanied with copious amounts of red wine. It would be a memorable meal and all of it homemade, of course, not by her. She was a crap cook but Mrs Stanhope down the street was a superb one.

As Sara pegged another black thong on the grubby plastic line, she smiled. She had been a big girl in her early twenties and could never have worn a thong. For one thing, she'd never have found it hidden amongst the rolls of fat. She wore big knickers in those days and owing to her size, had been the butt of many a joke.

In the black-and-gold decorated dining room, Sara set the table, a black-and-red theme. A vase of red roses took centre stage, their heady perfume scenting the air. The table had to have the wow factor in order to set the scene when Andy first entered the room. First impressions and all that, Sara thought, standing back to admire her handy work. She thought red was a seductive colour *and boy-oh-boy,* was she going to seduce Andy that night. When Sara seduced a man, they knew they'd been seduced and obviously loved it because they ran back for more.

She met Andy on line; she met all her prey on line. She trawled through many dating sites until the right man popped up and somehow she had a knack of searching out the right one after eliminating the detritus.

The smiling face of the dark-haired, well-built man, dressed smartly in a dark suit, appealed to Sara immediately. He looked damn good for fifty-eight. She had nodded approval at the monitor and thought, he'll do.

Their initial meeting took place in a swanky hotel near Birmingham. Andy had not been a letdown. He was exactly as he'd portrayed himself on the internet site. Some of the men Sara met were unattractive and looked nothing like their photograph, so she soon discarded them. After all, she did have standards. Although money was the main aim of the game, the man had to look good. Nothing worse than kissing a man with teeth missing and wrinkles you could float a boat in.

Andy had made her laugh from the moment they met. After several dates it was obvious he wasn't short of money by the way he lavished it on her. He took her to dine in posh restaurants, bought her gifts of perfume, silk underwear and clothes.

From the get-go, Sara had hung on Andy's every word, had fluttered her long lashes and had behaved coyly as though she were a young virgin and not a thirty-five year old tart who'd been round the block a time or two. Nevertheless, Andy appeared to lap it up and that was what mattered. Sara knew how to play this game. It was the fourth time of playing and she reckoned she would be up for an Oscar with her performances these days if she were a professional actor. She had perfect timing and knew when to give herself completely to a man. Each one thinking he was the first. This was her snare.

What man couldn't resist an attractive, red-haired woman with a gorgeous figure and alluring brown eyes? The one who said she was a lonely woman who simply longed for love. Had, in the past, been the victim of some awful men who had proved to want only sex from her and she was not giving up her virginity to the likes of those. No! She would only give herself to a man who proved he loved her. She would almost weep over the internet saying that her virginity was all she had to offer now. She had often wondered why men were stupid enough to believe it, but believe it they did. She had actually lost the virgin status when she was fifteen.

Her plan of action when meeting the new man in her life was to act shy but give him plenty of opportunities to ogle her fabulously improved tits, and always, always, let him make the decisions because men enjoy being in control. She was happy to let them think it while it suited her.

Sara put the final touches to her table arrangement by scattering silk rose petals haphazardly about the cloth. Then she quivered as Ben shot into her mind. He was her last victim, a polite man who knew how to treat a woman. At fifty-one, he was the youngest of her conquests and had stood out amongst other men. Although she had liked Ben, he had to go, but as he was a skilful lover, she did miss having sex with him when their affair was over.

Over for Sara was when the men in her life were skint. Usually by this time, *her* bank balance looked healthy but Ben wasn't as wealthy as the others she'd duped and within ten months, she had depleted his savings. She had dispatched him from her life as soon as he'd hinted his bank balance looked grim. He was out the door quicker than he'd entered. Sara had then started trawling the internet looking for another sap.

This was Andy. Tonight, she would give him what he craved. *Her*! She'd kept him at bay long enough. Poor man now gagged for it. She had wanted him to make love to her right off, but restraint was the name of the game. Could Andy give her the lifestyle she wanted?

Somehow, she knew he could. Therefore, after tonight, once he'd had her, he wouldn't want another woman. She'd then be able to dictate the terms of their relationship. Maybe, she might settle down with him. Get married. Perhaps it was time she devoted herself to one man, providing he had money of course.

That evening, Sara checked her appearance once more in the full-length mirror in her bedroom. Her black sequinned mini-dress just about covered her thighs and her staggeringly high red stilettos upped her height to five-feet-nine inches. Her false nails, varnished brilliant red, matched the colour on her lips. Turning sideways, she admired her reflection. She would do, she told herself, running her hands down her slender body. She looked like a vamp, exactly her intention.

Before leaving the bedroom, she smoothed the duvet, plumped the feather pillows then sprayed them with Chanel No 5. For good measure, she sprayed herself once more with it.

Downstairs, she checked on the food. It was keeping warm in the oven and the tiramisu keeping cool in the fridge. Bottles of white wine were on ice and the red breathing. Everything was set to go.

***

Andy was on his way, looking smart in a navy-blue suit. He strode along the pavement like a man who knew what was what. He did know *what was what*.

He'd met women like Sara before, women who fleeced men. Nonetheless, if she were going to relieve him of his hard-earned money, she'd have to work for it.

From their first meeting, everything about the way she behaved sent out signals for him to be wary. In spite of that, he liked her, so why not take a chance, he'd thought. It could be fun. Besides, she made heads turn and why not be in the company of a woman that other men found attractive? This thought had agreed with him. Although Andy had fancied the pants off Sara the moment he first saw her, he too could play the waiting game. The game would be over tonight though.

Heading to her front door, Andy told himself he had plenty of money now. He didn't need to swindle women anymore so why not spend the huge fortune he'd amassed on Sara. So long as she towed the line, did as told, and treated him with respect. Otherwise, she'd end up like the rest - at the bottom of his lake.

He knocked the door. Sara answered wearing a demure smile. Andy smiled back. "Good evening my love," he said, and then strode confidently into her house.

A Slice Of Life

"It was me who suggested it!" Doreen stated, placing two mugs of steaming tea on the kitchen table.

"Yes, I know. But you were joking," Ivy replied, rubbing her arthritic knee. "That's the problem with Anne. Suggest something and she goes and does it."

Doreen piled custard creams onto a willow patterned plate saying, "Too bad she didn't listen to us when we more than suggested she leave Tom."

Ivy nodded in agreement, then picked up her mug and took a sip, leaving a crimson red stain on the rim. "When you think about it," Ivy said, "Tom treated her terrible and kept her short of money so he could spend it on that floozy. I reckon he was seeing her for twenty years. Why the hell Anne put up with it I shall never understand."

Doreen reached for a biscuit. "I believe she stuck it out for the kids but even when they'd flown the nest, she stayed. It was only after Tom died Anne realized what she'd missed. I think that's why she's now letting her hair down. She's making up for lost time."

Ivy sniffed. "Huh! Maybe. Nevertheless, this is ridiculous, a woman her age doing that. She must be mad. Can't you tell her not to do it, Doreen?"

"I'm afraid you can't tell Anne anything these days. Remember when she told us she was going to do that bungee jump. I said, 'Don't be so daft. Do something less dangerous', and what does she go and do? A parachute jump. Talk about out of the frying pan and into the fire."

"I never thought she'd do it though," Ivy said. "I ask you. Seventy-four and jumps out of a plane."

Doreen shook her head and tutted. "Anne's just crazy."

Taking two biscuits from the plate, Ivy leaned back in her chair and began dunking them in her tea. Doreen watched mesmerized as Ivy managed to get the sodden biscuit into her mouth before it plopped back into the mug.

"I don't know how you can eat them that way and it makes the tea all slimy. Ooh… It's horrible," and Doreen shuddered at the thought of eating a soggy biscuit and drinking slimy tea.

"To my way of thinking it's the only way to eat a bicky," Ivy replied, taking another.

For a while, the two friends sipped their tea in silence until Doreen ended it. "Robert's going to decorate the kitchen for me," she said, glancing around the room. "It's time it was done. I've gone off this blue. I'm going to have sunshine yellow next."

"You're so lucky to have him, Doreen. My kids don't do a thing for me. It takes them all their time to visit so they wouldn't find time to decorate. If Harry were alive, he'd tell 'em a thing or two."

Doreen knew if Ivy dwelt on the subject of her

children, she'd do nothing but moan about them, so she decided to change the subject.

"Now, what are we going to do about Anne's latest idea?"

"It isn't an idea, she's gone and organised it," Ivy said.

"No! When?" Doreen sounded more than surprised.

"She won't tell me. Though I think it's next week. Mark my words, Doreen, she'll wish she hadn't done it the day after. Mind you, it takes a lot of nerve to do it."

Doreen drained the last of her tea then rose from the chair and winced. "Bugger! My hips giving me some stick today." She collected the empty mugs, hobbled to the sink and ran hot water into a bowl. "Ivy. Are we going on the outing next month?"

"If *you* want to go I'll go but I'm not keen on Weston."

Doreen screwed up her nose. "Me neither but it's better than staying in and if we both go, we'll be able to limp along the prom together." The two women laughed at that remark.

While Doreen washed and dried the mugs, Ivy ate biscuit after biscuit. While gobbling them down, she said, "The doctor told me last week if I lost weight my knee would improve. But honestly, I hardly eat a thing."

Doreen chuckled. "I noticed."

"Don't be sarcastic. That'll probably be all I'll eat

today."

Doreen put the tea towel over the Aga rail then went and sat opposite her life-long friend.

They had been silent for some time when Ivy announced, "It'll look nice yellow. Fresh looking. I could do with my kitchen painting but I don't have a son like Robert. He's a good lad. How old is he now?"

"He'll be fifty-four in June."

"Fifty-four," Ivy echoed. "Doesn't time fly? Of course, Anne's fortunate like you. Her Brian's wonderful. He pops in twice a week then collects her every Sunday and takes her to his house. My kids don't care if I'm alive or dead," Ivy moaned, twiddling with her pearl necklace.

Doreen waggled a finger in front of Ivy's face. "Now stop that kind of talk right now or you'll get depressed. Let's change the subject. What are we going to do about Anne?"

"We can't do anything, can we? Other than hope she survives and lives to tell the tale. If you ask me Anne gets dafter by the-"

The landline phone interrupted Ivy and Doreen waddled into the sitting room to take the call. Some minutes later, she returned.

"Ivy, we don't need to worry about Anne anymore. She's had it done and she's back home."

"Never!" Ivy stated, eyes bulging. "So what did she say about it?"

"She said having a face-lift is the best thing she's ever done, and listen to this, she's having liposuction on her belly as soon as she can."

"Goodness, Doreen, whatever will Anne think of doing next?"

Jonathan Harris

Jonathan Harris was sixty-five. His weekly trek into town took him fifty-three minutes. He could have caught a bus but he enjoyed the walk. With stout boots polished until they shone, Jonathan went into town every Thursday morning and as he strode there, excitement at what lay ahead grew with every step. His final destination was 'The Rest A While Hotel' but before reaching it, he popped into a local supermarket to buy a pint pot of plain yoghurt, which he wrapped in a plastic bag.

That particular Thursday, as Jonathan entered the foyer of the run down hotel his thoughts were not on resting a while, they were on who would conduct business in room twenty-three. He didn't need to introduce himself to the chap manning the reception desk. The ex boxer knew who he was and why he was there. He threw the key of room twenty-three at him saying, "Keep the noise down this week, will ya?"

***

Joan Smith was fifty-two, five-foot-three, chubby and round faced. She wore dowdy clothes and kept her greying hair extremely short. Joan juggled her time between her job and her demanding mother, a hypochondriac.

Joan felt suicidal that Thursday morning having listened to her mother moaning about how she never did anything right. Joan left for work wishing she had the nerve never to return home.

Arriving at the solicitor's office where she worked, her boss greeted her with, "Ah! There you are, Joan. I want you to run an errand for me today."

Joan looked at him, her eyes opening wide. Her boss only ever wanted her to work on accounts, now he wanted her to do something different, a change in her routine. Good! she thought.

Joan, excellent at her job, was worth more than her boss paid her. However, she undervalued herself and thought no one else would employ a plain woman who had never done anything more exciting than go to Bognor Regis for her holidays. Nevertheless, this was exciting. "An errand, Mr Jarvis? What about and where to?"

"It's to do with that unpaid bill of Mr Harris's and as I know where he'll be this lunchtime, I want this hand delivered to him." Mr Jarvis gave Joan a brown envelope. "And I've added interest. That'll get his attention because someone's told me he's a bit of a miser."

Joan cringed. "He won't get violent, will he, Mr Jarvis?"

"I shouldn't think so, Joan. Now, you'll find Mr Harris at 'The Rest A While Hotel'. I believe it's down a side street, somewhere by the library. I'm sure you'll find it."

At lunchtime, Joan set off on her errand. It was only when she entered the hotel that she realized she was carrying it out in her own time. Mr Jarvis is a skinflint, she thought, stepping over to the reception desk. He never mentioned paying me extra for doing this. "Excuse me. I'm looking for Mr Harris."

"Room twenty-three, love," said a voice from behind a newspaper.

"Thank you."

When Joan located room twenty-three, she hesitated before knocking the door.

"Bloody hell!" said the man who opened it. "You're old for this game, aren't you?"

"What game?" Joan asked, looking mystified.

"I hope you're good with a hairbrush?" he said.

"Oh, I see. You think I've come to do your hair. No. I'm from-"

"I know where you're from," he cut in. "So come in and get your coat off and we'll get started." He held up the pot of yoghurt. "I like it smeared over my belly and rubbed between my toes."

"Er… You are Mr J. Harris, aren't you?"

"Yes."

"Good, because you're the client I need to see," Joan said, stepping into the room and closing the door behind her. "Now, Mr Harris, I have something for-" Joan interrupted herself and couldn't believe her eyes. He'd taken off his trousers. "What on earth do you think you're doing, Mr Harris?"

"Well, it's no fun with your clothes on, now is it? So hurry up and get yours off."

"Mr Harris, I came here to give you this." Joan took the letter from her handbag and threw it at him. It landed on the dingy red carpet. "My boss wants you to-"

"I don't care what she wants," Mr Harris rudely interrupted. "I'll speak to her later and that letter is only to inform me she's upping her rates for the services of her girls. Look, I'm eager to get started. I'll fetch the hairbrush. I don't mind how hard you use it."

He disappeared into the bathroom leaving Joan gaping after him. She gathered her wits and bolted for the door. As she was about to open it, he called, "You know, you're not a bad looking filly. It's time they sent someone with a bit of meat on her bones. I reckon we'll be good together."

What stopped Joan leaving the room was that Mr Harris had actually taken notice of her. She knew he'd mistaken her for someone else but she was intrigued as to what he expected her to do. Therefore, she went and sat in a chair and waited for him to come out of the bathroom. When he emerged, hairbrush in hand, he was naked - except for his tartan socks. Joan stared at him, open-mouthed.

"I like my women to take my socks off for me."

"My word, Mr Harris, you do have some strange

fetishes."

Joan didn't smile at her remark but Mr Harris grinned at hearing it.

"Come on. Get those clothes off," he said, stepping towards her.

Joan sprang from the chair. "Now look here, Mr Harris. I'm not who you think I am. I'm not here to play with you. That letter," she pointed to it, "contains an unpaid bill, which you owe my boss."

"You mean you aren't from Madame Vera's beauty salon?"

"No! I'm Joan Smith from Browne and Browne."

Mr Harris gave his head a good scratch before saying, "Erm... I'm still game if you are?"

Joan mulled over his question. Perhaps there was a niche in this market for a dowdy woman. Perhaps she could do a bit of moonlighting during her lunch hour. She could release all the tension that had built up over the years by inflicting pain on someone willing to pay for it. Moreover, who would ever suspect her of doing naughty things in a hotel bedroom? No one, she convinced herself.

Braver than she ever thought possible, Joan asked, "How much do you pay? And what am I supposed to do?"

Mr Harris frowned. "Hmm... I'll pay you ninety-five quid for two hours because you're my kind of woman, but I don't want sex. I only want pleasure," he added with a smile.

"What do you call pleasure?"

"My yoghurt and hairbrush."

There was a knock at the door. Joan opened it and spoke with an attractive female in a tight red dress and red spike heels.

Closing the door with a bang, Joan said, "I think it's time for that pot of yoghurt, Mr Harris."

The Scarlet Thong

"So would you wear a thong?" Laura asked me, securing a blue one to the washing line with a peg, which looked bigger than the thong.

How any sensible woman can wear such underwear is beyond me. For one thing, thongs are uncomfortable.

I tried one once, for fun. While browsing the shops with my friend Samantha we wandered into a lingerie boutique. In the entrance, displayed in a basket, were scarlet thongs marked down to a pound each.

"I'm having one of those," Samantha said. "Are you?"

"You've got to be kidding," I replied, pulling one out of the basket and holding it up. "That wouldn't cover my bits."

After much cajoling, Samantha talked me into buying one.

"For a quid it'll be a laugh," I told the assistant while paying for it.

It amazes me that a bit of cloth can cost so much. These days, it seems the less material in a garment the more you pay. My knickers are substantial and cover my bits with a bit to spare and cost about two-fifty a pair.

Anyhow, my venture into a thong, just for a laugh, was... Hmm... Interesting. I didn't show it to my husband when I bought it. I decided to take it on holiday and surprise him. While packing the suitcase, I shoved it into the toe of one of my shoes. I didn't want him to see the thong yet.

On holiday, after a morning lazing on the beach, we went back to the hotel for our afternoon snooze. I showered and emerged from the bathroom wearing only the scarlet thong. "Ta-dah!" I sang, posing against the doorjamb. "What'cha think?"

For a moment, I could see he was stunned, and then he laughed.

"What the hell have you got on?"

"A thong," I told him, keeping my face straight and trying not to giggle.

"Give us a twirl then."

I twirled seductively and pouted like a vamp.

Trying to control his laughter by stuffing the sheet into his mouth, he ungraciously remarked, "Your love handles cover most of it."

"Huh! And here was I thinking I'd turn you on."

"You have. So come here."

I won't go into detail but it's enough to say we made love between outbursts of laughter. I still have the thong and take it on every holiday we spend together. After all, you need a good laugh now and then and anything that perks up your love life is okay by me, even my uncomfortable scarlet thong.

"*So would you wear a thong?*" Laura asked again, regaining my attention. "They've spiced up my love life no end."

"Don't be silly," I said, handing her another peg. "Are you forgetting I'm almost fifty-seven? I could never wear anything like that. Ever!"

I inwardly smiled at knowing I'd already packed my scarlet thong inside my suitcase. We're going on holiday next week and I'd be miffed if I forgot to pack it. After all, it's the little things in life that make you laugh!

Another Slice Of Life

Ivy dunked custard creams into her coffee and gobbled them down quickly. Doreen sat opposite her wondering if Ivy thought she was going to snatch the plateful of biscuits off the tea tray at any moment.

"And you have the nerve to say you're on a diet. Diet my arse. You've eaten four already."

"That's because I didn't have much breakfast and I feel peckish," Ivy said, reaching for another biscuit.

When she'd finished her coffee, she lowered herself almost into a sleeping position in Doreen's burgundy-coloured motorised armchair.

Doreen shuffled about trying to get comfortable in the normal armchair but couldn't, and to make matters worse, Ivy said, "Your Robert was ever so good to buy you this chair. It's comfortable and the way it supports my legs by the time I leave here they feel wonderful. I shall have to get myself one."

"I know it makes your legs feel good that's why I always sit in it. Except when you're here," Doreen added with a hint of annoyance in her voice.

As usual, Ivy took no notice. "So do you fancy coming to the tea dance?"

Doreen sighed. "I don't think so. I haven't danced for years and the way my hip is now, I'll look stupid limping around the floor."

"But like you've said before, Doreen, with your limp

and my arthritic knee we'll hobble around together. Oh! Francis says that new bloke from number twenty-six is coming. Apparently, he's a very pleasant man with lovely manners. Wouldn't you like to meet him?"

"I daresay I'll see him at the community centre so I don't have to go to the tea dance to meet him, unless it's you who wants to do that?" She looked at Ivy, who blushed and began fiddling with her pearl necklace. "I get the picture. You only want to drag me there so *you can* meet him."

"What's wrong with that?" Ivy asked, adjusting the chair into a sitting position. "He could be Mr Right. We might click."

Doreen laughed. "If he's like the rest of us, you will click. Click together as you dance round the floor."

Ivy frowned. "I don't understand."

Doreen didn't enlighten her but continued to chuckle at her mental vision of Ivy and the new man on the block, their hips and knees clicking as they wound their way round the dance floor.

Getting up, Doreen asked, "Want another drink?"

"I'll have a cuppa this time but I don't want any more biscuits."

"I shouldn't think so after polishing off half a plateful. You won't want any lunch."

"I don't eat lunch now. Since I started this new diet, I find I can last out until teatime."

Entering the kitchen, Doreen muttered, "I'm not

surprised seeing as you eat biscuit after biscuit during the day."

"What did you say?" Ivy demanded to know.

"Nothing. Just talking to myself."

Returning to the living room, Doreen set the tea tray down on a coffee table. "I've given it thought. I will go to the dance. It'll be a change from sitting here and Robert keeps telling me to get out more."

"You've a good son, Doreen."

Before Ivy could go on and on about her son who, according to Ivy, never lifted a finger to help her in any way, Doreen swiftly changed the subject.

"I've something to tell you about Anne."

Ivy sighed loudly. "So what's that woman done now?"

"She's met a man on the Internet and says she's going to meet him next Friday."

"Doreen, you've got to stop her. Hasn't she seen the news about perverts who pretend to be what they're not? She's asking for trouble arranging to meet a stranger at her age, whatever next?"

Doreen sat down with a thud and winced. "Bugger! That hurt."

Ivy hadn't heard or noticed. She was still going on about Anne's behaviour.

"The way Anne's carrying on these days I don't know what Tom would think if he was here now."

"That's good coming from you," Doreen snapped

back. "You're the first to say Tom was awful to her and when he died you said Anne was better off without him. Let's face it, if he was here now she still wouldn't have a life worth living. So if it makes her happy meeting men through the Internet, then let her get on with it is what I say."

Ivy sighed. "I can see trouble brewing. Anne's so compulsive."

"I agree with you, Ivy, but over the past few years she's done more than we have."

"Huh! You mean jumping from a plane and having a face-lift. I don't want to do any of those things thank you."

"Neither do I, but each to their own. If Anne gets pleasure doing way-out things then that's her business not ours. Anyway, before you get your knickers in a twist, it's Anne telling lies on the Internet. She's told the bloke she's sixty-two and she's going to see if she can get away with it."

"Never!" Ivy announced, reaching for her mug. "You'll have to talk to her or we'll be reading about her in the newspaper."

"That wouldn't surprise me one bit," Doreen said, offering Ivy a biscuit. She took two!

Best Friends?

We were in Karen's newly decorated green and red kitchen having coffee. As she was about to enter the pantry to fetch the biscuit tin, I said, "Dave's made a good job of the decorating and did you know he's having another affair?"

Karen returned with the tin, sat down with a thud on a chair then stared at me. She seemed to be finding it difficult to believe what she'd heard. I felt sorry for her but I always thought it was my place to inform her about her wayward husband. After all, what are best friends for?

Karen and I have known one another thirty years. Dave has always been a flirt and although he treats Karen well, he's had numerous affairs. She always tells me about them but this time I think she had no inkling he'd embarked on another.

"Do you know who it is?" she asked.

"No." I lied. I felt my face grow red and sipped my coffee hoping she hadn't noticed.

"So, do you know how long this one's been going on?"

"Two months," I told her.

Karen tutted. "I can't believe I haven't noticed. I usually pick up on little things he does that give the game away."

We drank the remainder of our coffee in silence. I

guessed Karen was mulling over how to approach Dave in order to tell him she knew about his latest affair.

In the past, I'd always been her shoulder to cry on and offered her comfort and understanding. To be fair to Dave though there were times when Karen pushed him too far. When they married, twenty years or so ago, she tried keeping him on a tight leash and short of money. I tried telling her then not to as Dave was not the kind of man to put up with it. They argued for years about his going out to the pub or the snooker hall. Karen didn't enjoy either activity so wouldn't go with him. It wasn't long before he met a woman and started his first fling. It only lasted a few weeks but, as they say, once a man has a roving eye it keeps roving. Mind you, Karen's constant moaning at him didn't help. If it wasn't one thing, it was another. I suppose, thinking about it, Dave had a rough time with her. Still, when you're married, you're married.

Karen stood up. "Want another coffee?"

"Yes, please."

Placing two mugs of steaming coffee on the table, Karen said, "I know I've asked you this before but if your Pete had played around would you have divorced him?"

"Yes! I would. I told him right from the day we married if he was ever unfaithful I'd leave him and never return. I meant it too. Once you've lost the trust, it's gone. Thankfully, he never went astray."

"How do you know he didn't?"

"Because if he'd had another woman, I'd have cottoned on instantly."

"You mean you think you would have."

"No! I'm certain I would have."

"There's only one certainty in life, Fay, and that's death." Karen stared at the kitchen wall for a couple of moments then gave a huge sigh. "You know, I've only ever truly loved one man and he will always be the love of my life. What's more, I knew he loved me but he wouldn't leave his wife. He didn't want to lose his children. He adored them you see. Our affair lasted years and no one ever knew."

I was flabbergasted at what I'd heard. Little stay at home Karen had had an affair. It was unbelievable.

I was about to push for more information but Karen said, "You do know who Dave's seeing, don't you?"

I couldn't lie again, so I told her. "Yes. It's Dawn Casey."

"Ah! So that's who he ditched you for, is it?"

I gulped and didn't know what to say. My best friend knew about my having an affair with her husband. How do you deal with a statement like that? I just stared at the table feeling uncomfortable and ashamed.

"So, are you going to ask me how I knew about you and Dave?"

"Did *he* tell you?" I said.

"He didn't have to," Karen replied, reaching for a chocolate biscuit from the tin. "He came home at times reeking of your perfume. And when he was out, you were too. It was obvious, Fay. There were times when I wanted to tell you I knew about you and him, because every time we met you not only looked guilty you seemed uncomfortable in my presence."

It was the first time I'd had an affair and why I chose to have one with Dave, I shall never know. I shall regret it forever because you don't have an affair with your best friend's husband, do you? My only excuse is that since Pete's death, I'd been lonely and needed a man's company. Dave happened to be on hand, but like all his other conquests, he dumped me after a few months and moved on to Dawn.

I stood up and pushed back my chair. "I'd better go and I doubt I'll be welcome here again. I'm sorry, Karen."

"Don't be so daft. Sit down and have a biscuit. Dave will never change and frankly, I don't give a damn anymore. As long as he keeps paying the bills and lets me do as I want, I can live with it. Besides, we all have secrets and as we are having a tell the truth day, I'm going to *tell you* something. Your Pete did have an affair."

"Pete? But he never went out at night without me."

"That's because he saw her during the day."

I felt my heart drop. "Are you telling me the truth,

Karen? Or are you saying this just to hurt me?"

"Fay, you're my best friend. I wouldn't lie about a thing like that."

I felt a little stupid. Pete had deceived me and I'd not known about it. I couldn't take it in but I knew by Karen's expression that she was telling the truth. "So... who was she?" I asked.

"Me!" Karen announced. "And as I said earlier, Pete was the love of my life."

The Bride

Many hundreds of years ago, at the confluence of two rivers, a large settlement thrived. The river water ran deep and clean and fish was plentiful. Along the banks, willow trees provided fuel for fires.

Sporadic raiding from other tribes was a threat to the village but the angle formed by the two rivers made a natural defence. It was awkward to get at but easily defended, so the village did not suffer much from marauders.

This was in the time where on moonlit nights, villagers sat in front of their longhouses listening to the elders telling stories. Warmed by a crackling fire they listened intently to every word. Sometimes they shivered at the blood curdling tales and laughed loudly at the comical ones.

They enjoyed mythical tales the most and the one about the land of the dead, which lay many miles to the east of the village, was a particular favourite. The story went like this.

A young woman named Orla longed to be married. She was a beauty with silky flaxen hair that reached her waist and her skin was soft and flawless. She was the daughter of the richest man in the village but he was selfish and wanted to keep Orla for himself. Many men had offered jewels and livestock to marry her but Orla's father, who had no need of more wealth, turned down all her suitors.

Orla pleaded with him. "Please, Father, allow me to marry. All the women in the village of my age are now married." Nonetheless, no amount of tears helped her cause.

The day came when the son of a respected elder travelled far in order to ask for Orla's hand in marriage but her father rejected him. The elder felt his son and family were dishonoured by the refusal so as he understood the spirit world, he cast a spell on Orla's father. He had to accept the next suitor who asked for Orla's hand, no matter who he was or where he came from.

One night, Orla heard singing coming from the river. She rose from her goatskin-covered bed and ran to the river's edge to see many small boats making their way towards her village. Men in the crafts held pitch-wood torches to light their way.

Concealing herself behind a tree, Orla watched as they drew near and saw that a number of boats contained goods. Some filled with intricately woven rugs, others filled with wooden chests, their lids open, exposing gold coins and trinkets and on one boat, goats and pigs jostled for space.

A tall, dark-haired young man, wearing a bright red robe, stepped from the largest boat as it pulled up beside the riverbank.

"Unload the cargo and take it to the house of Orla's

father," he told his followers.

Hearing the commotion, Orla's father came outside and couldn't believe what he saw. He'd never seen such wealth.

The suitor's name was Gudmond. He carried himself proud and had a look that commanded respect. Within hours, Orla's father had consented to the marriage between Gudmond and Orla. Her father couldn't fathom why he had felt compelled to give his consent, because he still wanted to keep Orla for himself.

That same night, Gudmond and Orla bid her father goodbye then began making their way back to Gudmond's village. Throughout the journey, Orla felt bewitched and couldn't keep awake longer than a second or two. She had no idea her journey had lasted two days.

When they arrived at Gudmond's village, it was dark. Although the hour was late, the people greeted her warmly. Her new village was far superior to her old one. The longhouses were more spacious and circled a huge fire, where five suckling pigs roasted on a spit.

After the feast, Orla and Gudmond retired to his longhouse, where they made love for hours on layers of fur. Finally, Orla fell into a contented sleep, snuggling close to her husband.

She woke late the next day and heard no sound. Not even a bird singing but there was a dreadful smell of decaying flesh. Orla turned to face Gudmond and her screams rang through the village but no one came to her aid. Gudmond had turned into a rotting corpse.

Orla ran from the house to find more bodies in various stages of decay. Crying with fright, she raced to the river. Her intention was to jump into a boat and paddle away as fast as she could but when she reached them, they were rotten and useless.

She looked around and in the distance saw smoke curling into the sky. She set off in its direction and eventually came upon an old woman sat before a fire. Falling to her knees, Orla told the wizened woman her story. As she listened, she nodded knowingly.

"My child," she said tenderly, when Orla had finished speaking, "you are in the land of the dead. You can never leave. My suitor also tricked me and I have lived here many years. But I will tell you the ways of this land."

The old woman poked at the fire before continuing.

"You must sleep during the day and wake when it's dark. Only then will the people of the village be flesh and blood. They carry a curse for angering a powerful mystic many years ago. At night, they will behave as when they were alive. At dawn, they rot and turn into skeletons. You must now return to the village and sleep. If you do not, when your husband wakes he will seek you out. Tonight when you wake, all will be well."

Orla returned to the village and adapted herself to the

ways of her new life.

Ten months later, she gave birth to a son who remained flesh and blood throughout daylight. He was the first child born normal since the curse. Everyone was pleased, especially Gudmond. In spite of that, because granted a normal life, the child had to live amongst his own kind. The elders told Orla she had to take him back to her village.

Orla, saddened to leave Gudmond for she truly loved him, knew her son could not grow up in the land of the dead. She bid Gudmond farewell and a group of elders escorted her back to her village.

On the way, an elder said, "I have just had a vision, Orla. When you reach your father's house, you must not take your son out of his cradle for five days and nights. This will ensure he remains flesh and blood until the day he dies."

Orla waved goodbye to the elders and watched them sail away until they were out of sight.

She then went to seek out her father. As they sat by the fire warming their hands, she told him all her news, especially the elder's warning that her child must remain in his cradle for five days and nights.

Three days later, while Orla was collecting firewood, a friend came to visit. Hearing the baby crying, she lifted him from his cradle to comfort him but as she did, the flesh started to fall from his body. She threw him back into his cradle and ran screaming from the house.

When Orla returned her son was a pile of tiny bones. She wept for hours over the cradle but that night her son became flesh and blood once more. Orla knew if the people of her village found out they would banish them. So she returned to the land of the dead, knowing she could never leave, but she was happy her son would grow up with his own kind.

Yet Another Slice Of Life

"Get yourself into a chair before you bust a gut," Doreen joked, closing the front door.

"Blimey! I haven't heard that saying for years," Ivy replied, making her way into the living room. "And yes, I could do with a sit down. I've been on the go all morning."

Doreen headed into the kitchen to prepare coffee. "Are you taking sugar this week?" she called.

"Yes, two spoonfuls, and I'll have a couple of custard creams."

Doreen hobbled back into the living room with its bold yellow-and-black wallpaper. Ivy sat in the burgundy-coloured motorised armchair, her legs outstretched. Why does she always make a beeline for my chair? Doreen thought. She knows I can't get comfortable on the sofa. Trying to keep irritation from her voice and failing to do so, she said, "Your diet didn't last long, Ivy, did it?"

"No, and I blame Anne. You know me, when I'm worried about something I eat and eat. And since Anne told us she was getting married, I've been so worried over it, I haven't been able to stop eating."

Doreen winced as she dropped onto the sofa. "Bugger! This hip's painful today. I'll have to see the doctor again."

"Me too!" Ivy announced, rubbing her arthritic knee.

"Getting old's a pain isn't it?"

"Yes, and I now have to get up again because the kettle's boiled." Doreen rose unsteadily from the sofa and hobbled into the kitchen.

She returned carrying a tray that held two mugs of milky coffee and a plate piled high with custard creams. She placed the tray on a small table between the sofa and the motorised armchair.

Reaching for her coffee and a custard cream, Ivy said, "Don't you think Anne's mad getting married? Then again, she is mad. What with bungee jumping, parachuting, facelifts and liposuction, she's one crazy woman."

Plonking down on the sofa, Doreen replied, "Good luck to her is what I say. Why shouldn't she marry Martin? He treats her better than Tom ever did. She's entitled to a bit of happiness."

"I'm not saying she isn't but I don't think she's thought it through. I bet she hasn't thought of..." Ivy trailed off and Doreen sensed a delicate matter was on the tip of Ivy's tongue.

"Thought of what?" Doreen prompted.

Ivy whispered, "Her wedding night. Martin will expect sex. He's the type."

Doreen chuckled. "Ivy Mason, you're so old fashioned. They've been having sex for months."

Ivy looked gobsmacked. "They haven't, have they? At their age? Never! You don't think she's daft enough to get married in a wedding dress, do you?"

"Ah! I'm glad you brought that up. Anne wants me to ask you if you'll be a bridesmaid with me. She's set her mind on having a traditional wedding. She never had one with Tom and you know Anne's view on age. You're never too old for anything. She's going the whole hog. Ten yards of tulle, tiara, long veil and wants me and you in pink bridesmaid dresses."

"Doreen, that woman's lost her marbles. If she thinks I'm going to wear a bridesmaid dress at my age, she can think again. In any case, what will we look like? Imagine the pair of us limping up the aisle with the aid of a walking stick."

Doreen laughed. "At least the congregation won't see our bunions. Our long pink dresses will cover them up."

Ivy bristled. "No. I won't do it, Doreen."

"Don't do it then! Let's change the subject. Did you tell Rose I'll be going on the trip to Weston?"

"Yes," Ivy said, dunking her custard cream into her coffee.

This irritated Doreen because occasionally Ivy missed her mouth and the biscuit plopped back into the mug causing coffee to splash over the chair.

With a soggy biscuit poised an inch from her red lips, Ivy added, "But you've got to pay the deposit by tomorrow."

"I will," Doreen replied, mentally willing Ivy to open

her mouth and pop in the biscuit. Ivy did open her mouth, a fraction too late and the biscuit dropped into the mug.

"Bother! I'm always doing that." Ivy brushed splashes of coffee from her grey sweater.

"Yes, *you are* always doing that," Doreen snapped back.

A few uncomfortable moments slipped by before Doreen said, "Have a look at my kitchen before you go. Robert's finished it now. It looks lovely. It's kind of bluey-grey and I've managed to-"

"You said you were having it painted yellow," Ivy rudely interrupted."

"I changed my mind."

"You mean Robert changed it for you."

"No he didn't."

"I bet he did."

"Oh, have it your way," Doreen said, a touch of anger in her voice. "You always have to get in the last word whatever I say."

After their altercation, an embarrassing silence set in. Ivy twiddled with her imitation pearl necklace and Doreen stared out of the window. When Doreen's mobile phone rang, it immediately eased the tension between them.

Doreen pulled the phone from her trouser pocket and looked at caller display.

"It's Anne," she said, answering the phone. "Hello,

Anne. Are you..." was all she managed to utter because Anne had on her nattering head and Doreen couldn't get another word in.

"Er..." Doreen tried interrupting but trying to stop Anne when she was in full flow was near impossible. "Er..." she tried again then raised her voice. "Anne! Will you please shut up. Ivy's here and she said she'd love to be your bridesmaid."

"No I didn't!" Ivy shouted.

"Okay, Anne, we'll discuss it tonight. Bye!"

Before Doreen had time to replace the phone into her pocket, Ivy said, "I am not wearing a bridesmaid dress and that's that!"

"Ivy, you'd believe anything. I've been having you on. You didn't really think Anne was getting married in a wedding dress, did you? Give the woman a little credit. She's ordered a pale-blue suit and a matching hat and said she wants us to be matrons of honour. We can wear what we like and in any colour. So, what sort of outfit shall we treat our self to? A dress or a suit?"

Ivy frowned. "Dunno... But to tell you the truth, I was beginning to warm to the idea of wearing a pink bridesmaid dress."

The Murder of Gareth Hughes

Charlotte Chambers, journalist for the local newspaper 'Your News', sat listening to Olivia Walter's confession on Olivia's brown leather sofa in her living room.

Olivia had telephoned the newspaper office the day before asking to speak with Charlotte. When she took the call, Olivia confessed to the murder of a man discovered on waste ground on the outskirts of Tamworth. At that time, the police were still trying to identify him as no personnel effects were found on the body.

***

Charlotte had reported on the murder three days previously. When Olivia first spoke to Charlotte, Olivia had said, "This isn't a hoax and to prove it, ask the police if the postmortem revealed a large quantity of sleeping pills in the man's stomach."

Intrigued by what Olivia had told her, Charlotte reported it to her boss.

At first, he was sceptical. All sorts of odd balls crawled out of the woodwork admitting to the crime of murder in an ongoing investigation. Still, he would call the local Detective Inspector. Much to his surprise and off the record, the detective admitted sleeping tablets were present in the stomach contents of the deceased.

Charlotte then had the go-ahead to interview Olivia

Walter and offer her money for her story. If it were true, it would make national news and Charlotte saw herself moving from the provincial newspaper to a mainstream one.

***

"So is that it, Olivia? Have you told me the entire story?" Charlotte asked, looking up from her notepad, where she had more or less jotted down everything Olivia had said. "Explain again though, why you wanted him dead."

Olivia let out an exasperated sigh. "I've already told you."

"I know you have but I'd like to hear it again. After all, you made it quite clear that before you went to the police you wanted the facts known. If what you're telling me is true, you'll be paid two-hundred grand for this story, so I need to get *my* facts right. So, tell me again, right from the moment you and Sally plotted his death."

Olivia Walter came across as a hard woman who hadn't shown remorse about killing Gareth Hughes. In fact, she kept repeating it was what he deserved. Two women had snuffed out his life because they wanted to teach him a lesson for two-timing them, and thirty-four year old Olivia Walter had been the instigator of the crime.

Olivia cleared her throat then began her story once more.

Charlotte listened intently, checking her notes to make sure Olivia didn't alter her earlier story. Charlotte knew people who lied needed a good memory. Either Olivia Walter had a good one or she had told the truth because she hadn't uttered a word differently.

Olivia's account of things went like this.

***

She sat alone one Tuesday morning having a coffee in Costa's in Tamworth when a woman entered crying. A dog running loose had tripped her over and she'd cut her knee. Shaken, the woman came into Costa's to calm down over a coffee.

Olivia went to her aid asking if she could do anything. The woman, Sally Green, said she'd be fine in a minute or two but Olivia insisted she join her at her table.

Sally did, and it seems she and Olivia started chatting and over coffee, Sally produced photographs of her fiancé. Olivia did a double take of several photographs then realized she stared at her own fiancé, or at least someone who resembled him.

"Has he a twin brother?" Olivia asked.

"No. But why do you want to know?"

Olivia opened her purse and pulled out a photograph saying, "Because I think your fiancé and mine is one of the same."

For a while, Sally had stared open-mouthed studying

the photo before shouting, "It can't be!"

Several customers in the coffee shop had turned their attention on them.

"Keep your voice down," Olivia had ordered.

The two women then compared notes and were of the opinion their fiancé was the same man and leading them, as the saying goes, up the garden path, with no intention of marrying either.

Sally was heartbroken to find Gareth had been unfaithful, whereas Olivia was enraged at him for two-timing her. Therefore, as Olivia saw it, the two-timing dirt-bag had to go.

Olivia had always accepted Gareth, a steel erector earning good money, worked in Leeds from Monday until Friday night and only able to come home at weekends. Sally believed Gareth worked in various locations from Friday morning to Monday night and only able to live with her for the remainder of the week. It was pure luck the two women met that day and couldn't believe they hadn't bumped into each other while out with Gareth, particularly as they only lived fifteen miles apart.

Leaving the coffee shop, the two women had agreed to murder him the following Saturday.

***

During that Saturday, Olivia laced his food and drink with sleeping tablets and, eventually, they worked. By nine o'clock that evening, he was out for the count.

Olivia rang Sally and when she arrived at Olivia's flat, they held a pillow over Gareth's face until he died. Body full of sleeping tablets prevented him from struggling.

After killing him, they rolled him in a carpet then during the cover of darkness carried him outside and shoved him onto the back seat of Olivia's land rover. She then drove to waste ground, four miles from Tamworth, where they dumped his body.

***

"So, Olivia, why did you want to tell *me* about it? We both know if you'd gone to a mainstream newspaper, you'd receive more money than my paper is offering. A woman confessing to murder and knowing the facts is front-page news. Don't get me wrong, it's a once in a lifetime opportunity for a small-town journalist like me and I am grateful. Still, why *me*?"

"Because you deserve it."

"Why's that?" Charlotte asked, coming to the end of a page in her notepad and turning over to the next.

"Because didn't Gareth take you to court and receive half your assets when he left you after six years?"

Looking surprised at Olivia's revelation, Charlotte said, "How do *you* know about it?"

"Because I overheard him tell someone it wouldn't be long before he was screwing me out of my money just like he had done with Charlotte Chambers, so I did a little investigating. When I discovered he'd sued you for half your estate and presumably was about to do the same to me, I decided to kill him. You see, I came into an inheritance a couple of years back and I'm now quite wealthy. No way was I going to let that dirt-bag get a penny of it. I wasn't letting a confidence trickster sue me in court. My meeting Sally was pure chance and I had no idea he was living with her when not living with me. As I see it, Charlotte, we've rid the world of a man who preys on women and when the jury hear Sally's sob story, and mine, we'll get the sympathy vote. We could be out of prison in six years. Then Sally and I will enjoy spending my inheritance. Plus the money your newspaper will pay me for my story."

Charlotte closed her notepad, stood up from the sofa and while heading for the door, said, "My boss will deposit the money into your bank account when all you've told me is substantiated. Thank you, Olivia."

"You're welcome," she replied, picking up her mobile.

As Charlotte closed the door behind her, she suspected Olivia was ringing the police to confess to the murder of thirty-eight year old Gareth Hughes.

Yes, she's right, Charlotte thought. The two-timing dirt-bag did deserve it, and making her way to her car, she started whistling.

A Fairy Story

Long ago, when fairies whispered in trees and their mischief touched almost everyone, Edward, an earl's son and a gallant knight, went into his father's forest of oak and ash one morning to hunt. He never returned. Stories circulated throughout the countryside that a Fairy Queen had captured Edward and he was now under her spell.

Edward wasn't the first knight to disappear in that forest, and legend told that only a maiden with an innocent heart could save a knight who'd been bewitched by a Fairy Queen. Edward could only return to his former life if a maiden loved him enough to conquer the Fairy Queen's hold on him.

The rescue of a mortal from the grasp of fairies was dangerous. Few people had the courage to attempt one. Not Rosalind though. She was a fair maiden with golden hair and bright blue eyes.

Rosalind lived in a castle and was a handmaiden to the queen of the county. Rosalind had heard that a knight, who'd been bewitched, guarded the forest and she longed to meet him. The forest was a mile from the castle but the queen had forbidden any of her subjects to venture into it. Rumour was that the knight patrolled it by day looking for intruders. When he saw one, he called to the fairies by way of a magic flute. When they came, they captured the intruder and him or her, never seen again.

One afternoon, Rosalind left the castle and without thinking, wandered into the forest. She was about to pick sweet-smelling honeysuckle to weave in her hair, when a dark haired knight appeared. He stood before her, tall and proud, cloaked in emerald green and royal blue silk. "I am Edward," he said, giving her a bow.

Rosalind fell in love with him the instant her eyes met his and because he fell in love with her, he didn't summon the fairies. Rosalind and Edward remained together until dusk. It had been a joyous time and when Rosalind left the forest that evening, she was no longer an innocent maiden.

She returned to the forest the following afternoon to find Edward waiting for her. As they lay on a carpet of primrose and cowslip, he told Rosalind his story.

He had lost his way in the forest that fateful day and had stopped to rest his horse. He'd dismounted then lain down on the grass and closed his eyes to the sunshine. He was fast asleep when a sweet voice roused him. When he opened his eyes, the Fairy Queen was bending over him, smiling. Held spellbound by her beauty, Edward was unable to move. She kissed him and that act had bound him to her. She led him deep into the forest, their steps hushed by moss, the scent of bramble rose, heavy on the air.

Since captured by the Fairy Queen, Edward had served her faithfully for he was unable to break the spell she had cast over him. The spell that meant he must do everything she asked of him. Moreover, he could never leave the forest and live with mortals again until a mortal woman loved him above all other.

On Midsummer Eve, Rosalind left the castle and went into

the forest of oak and ash to carry out the instructions Edward had given her. She went to a crossroad and hid behind a hedge.

At midnight, in the distance, she heard flutes and harps playing softly. The exquisite sound grew louder. Then into view came a column of fairies riding pure white horses, their bridles jingling with gold and silver bells. At the head rode the Fairy Queen dressed in silver and white gossamer, her red hair cascading down her back. At the rear of the troop rode Edward.

As he drew alongside Rosalind, she put his plan into action. She sprang from her hiding place and pulled him from his horse.

Instantly, the fairies cried out, "Majesty! Majesty! A mortal has captured Edward."

The queen reigned in her horse, swivelled in her saddle and gave Rosalind an icy stare. For a moment, Rosalind faltered, but the love she had for Edward gave her the courage and strength to continue. She wrapped her arms around him and clutched him to her. Rosalind knew the Fairy Queen would now do her magic so she ordered herself to be brave.

With a quickness she hadn't expected, Edward changed into a serpent but Rosalind's hold on him didn't slacken because Edward had said that only a mortal's grasp could save him from the Fairy Queen's spell.

The Fairy Queen shouted and the serpent grew huge. It coiled itself around Rosalind and started squeezing the life out of her delicate body. Yet Rosalind repeatedly told it, "I love you, Edward. I will love you forever."

For several minutes, Rosalind battled with the serpent, her strength ebbing away but somehow she clung onto the vile creature. The Fairy Queen tried to steady her prancing white stallion but it was terrified of the creature and refused to obey his mistress. Unable to control her horse, the Fairy Queen screeched in anger then galloped away, followed by her fairy troop. Seconds later, they faded into the forest.

Rosalind, exhausted from the struggle, sank onto the soft earth weeping for Edward who seemed to have disappeared, but then, she heard a footstep break a twig.

Looking up, she saw Edward coming towards her. She quickly rose to her feet and ran to greet him. Edward, stripped of his finery was weak from his battle with Rosalind. She took off her scarlet cloak and wrapped it around his naked body. Then they lay on sweet-smelling clover until Edward regained his strength.

Later, hand in hand, they left the forest of oak and ash vowing never to return, their love for one another now steadfast and true.

No Rival

Slowly, Maria bent to check Simon's pulse. He lay on the cinema car park.

"Daniel, you've killed him."

"He had it coming. Serves him right," Daniel replied, running a hand through his blond hair.

"But I didn't think you'd kill him."

"Then he shouldn't have touched you up."

"Daniel, it was nothing. I only told you about it for a laugh. Why do you get so jealous? You know I only love you."

"Then you shouldn't lead other guys on."

"It's just for fun, that's all. Christ! You do realize what you've done?… Daniel! Are you listening to me? I said, you do realize what you've done?"

Of course, he knew what he had done. He'd thought about it night and day for the past two weeks. The petite, dark-haired, twenty-eight-year-old Maria was his reason for living. Without her, there would be no point in carrying on, no reason to rise each morning and struggle through the day. She was his rock, his anchor. He'd be adrift without her. Yeah, Daniel knew what he had done and he would do it again. He'd already got rid of John and Phil. Every time a guy got too close to Maria, he dealt with them.

Staring at one another across Simon's body, the knife hanging loosely in Daniel's hand and still dripping with blood, Maria said, "We'll have to get rid of him."

They bundled Simon's body into the boot of her black four-by-four, covered it with a tartan rug, drove to Cannock Chase and stopped in a secluded wooded area.

"We'll have to bury him deep," Maria said as they lifted Simon's body from the boot. "We don't want him discovered."

Daniel fell to his knees and began digging Simon's grave. A sturdy, oak branch made a makeshift spade. The ground, baked hard by the absence of rain, made digging difficult but gradually, Daniel's task became less strenuous as firm ground gave way to softer earth.

When the grave was deep enough to hide Simon's body, they heaved him in.

After covering the corpse with earth, Daniel patted the ground flat then littered the gravesite with dry leaves and debris. No one would ever have guessed the earth below concealed a six foot, well-built man.

Daniel and Maria finally headed back to Tamworth, locked in their own thoughts.

Maria's were on Steven, a new guy at the office. She would soon have him under her spell.

Daniel sat quietly thinking of Maria. He now had no rival for her love. That love, so strong a power that he would kill for her, was safe - at present.

Goodbye

That afternoon we drank red wine
Made love.
Drifting down from ecstasy
I looked into her eyes.
Eyes once full of love
Now misty and sad.
When she told me
We cried.
Opening the door
She mouthed goodbye.
Goodbye I said in return
And she was gone.
Pillow soaked with tears
I left the hotel room to face life without her.

Late for Church

They lie in a field of clover, its perfume scenting the air.
When he kisses her, she yields to temptation,
And hears a distant bell.
They are late for church.
With her Sunday dress stained with grass,
His breeches grubby at the knee,
They run hand in hand until under the lych-gate,
They part with a kiss.
Now too late for church.
He heads for the big house; she goes to collect her pails.
But next Sunday in that field of clover,
They will dally and be once more,
Too late for church.

Forever Girl

He told me I was his forever girl,
Forever and ever.
When he gave me flowers on my birthday,
anniversary,
He told me I was his forever girl.
He wept when our children were born,
And told me I was his forever girl.
While I nursed him back to health,
He whispered you're my forever girl.
One day my forever boy didn't come home.
Now he tells another she is his forever girl.
And my forever boy is lost to me.

She remembers George Henry

She lies in a field dotted with poppies.
Looking up she watches fluffy clouds roll by.
Some form shapes as they go.
A lion. A dragon. Reminds me of my mother, he says.
And she laughs.
Leaning on his elbow, he stares into her eyes.
I love you, Jenny.
Love you too, she replies, bringing him to her.
They make love to the sound of skylarks and the buzz
of bumblebees.
Drifting down from ecstasy, tears in her eyes, she
reaches for him.
But knows the dream is shattered.
George is gone. Gone to war.
To die in the trenches.

Thank you for reading my collection of short stories. I hope you enjoyed them. A review on Amazon would be welcome. Best wishes and happy reading from me to you.

Copyright 2016.©

Perhaps you would enjoy reading one of my novels.

'Hannah Kimble' is set in 1946 in a quaint English village. A story of love and betrayal between a charismatic American wartime pilot and a lonely dowdy English woman.

'No Reserve On Love' A modern day romance that develops a darker side.

'In Dangerous Company' A contemporary romantic suspense.

Printed in Great Britain
by Amazon